The Annethology

A Collection of Kindred Spirits

INSPIRED BY THE CANADIAN ICON

ISBN: 9781773661537

Printed in Canada

Designed by Tracy Belsher
Compiled by Judith Graves
Edited by Robin Sutherland

Library and Archives Canada Cataloguing in Publication

Title: The Anne thology : a collection of kindred spirits inspired by the Canadian icon / stories compiled by Judith Graves ; edited by Robin Sutherland. Other titles: Anne thology (2024) | Annethology Names: Graves, Judith, compiler. | Sutherland, Robin, 1968- editor. Identifiers: Canadiana (print) 20240309979 | Canadiana (ebook) 20240314093 | ISBN 9781773661537 (softcover) | ISBN 9781773661544 (EPUB) Subjects: LCSH: Shirley, Anne (Fictitious character)—Juvenile fiction. | LCSH: Short stories, Canadian—21st century. | CSH: Short stories, Canadian (English)—21st century. | LCGFT: Short stories. Classification: LCC PS8321 .A56 2024 | DDC jC813/.0108351—dc23

The publisher acknowledges the support of the Government of Canada, the Canada Council for the Arts and the Province of Prince Edward Island for our publishing program.

ACORNPRESS

P.O. Box 22024
Charlottetown, Prince Edward Island
C1A 9J2
acornpresscanada.com

The *Anne* THOLOGY

A Collection of Kindred Spirits

INSPIRED BY THE CANADIAN ICON

Stories compiled by Judith Graves

Edited by Robin Sutherland

30 YEARS

ACORNPRESS

*Celebrating thirty years of
Island stories and voices.*

CONTENTS

Introduction	.....	1
Anne and the Bloody Book	.....	4
by Susie Moloney		
In Search of Kindred Spirits	.....	31
by Hope Dalvay		
Carpetbaggers	.....	64
by Paul Coccia		
4624463	.....	89
by Natasha Deen		
The Wooden Box	.....	128
by Deirdre Kessler		
Anne of the Silver Trail	.....	151
by Shari Green		
Anne, from nowhere in particular	.....	195
by Matthew Dawkins		
Where the Dark Goes	.....	214
by Mere Joyce		
Matthew Insists on Ripped Jeans	.....	240
by Susan White		
ANNe	.....	270
by Judith Graves		

INTRODUCTION

"There's such a lot of different Annes in me. I sometimes think that is why I'm such a troublesome person. If I was just the one Anne it would be ever so much more comfortable, but then it wouldn't be half so interesting."

So decides Anne Shirley, the red-haired young orphan whose unexpected arrival at Green Gables brings great joy—and more than one headache—to the hearts and home of Matthew and Marilla Cuthbert.

Anne, of course, is the feisty heroine of Lucy Maud Montgomery's well-loved Canadian classic, *Anne of Green Gables*, and her universal desire to belong has spanned generations, cultures, and continents. The Anne series has been translated into over 36 languages, adapted for film and television, and has inspired many other works of fiction and graphic novels. Many loyal fans have also visited the red sand roads of Prince Edward Island to

explore the real-life places of Anne's fictional world.

Whip-smart and wildly imaginative, *Anne of Green Gables* has always inspired readers to see the possibilities in the mundane, to test boundaries, and to ask difficult questions about who they are and who they want to be.

With that in mind, who's YOUR Anne?

We posed this question to ten Canadian young adult fiction writers, challenging them to work with characters, plots, themes, and details from the original *Anne of Green Gables* story, but in new and innovative ways.

The ANNEthology is the result of this query, and has produced a dynamic collection of short stories and poetry that explores issues most relevant to contemporary readers of all ages. Meet these modern Annes as they navigate foster care, mining town, high-school cafeteria, and haunted house, all with the customary pluck and vivid imagination that you love and expect of a true Anne.

If that isn't enough scope for your imagination, consider an unexpected journey with an obese gay male Anne in search of home, or a Jamaican Anne caught up in the world of child trafficking.

And be sure to catch your breath and hold on to your straw hats and carpetbags for your encounter with a killer AI Anne out for redemption, a futuristic rebel Anne conspiring to save books. . .or an Anne who trades her soul for a good read and her heart's desires.

"Kindred spirits are not so scarce as I used to think."

2024 marks the 150th anniversary of L. M. Montgomery's birth and, as fate would have it, the 30th anniversary of Acorn Press, Prince Edward Island's longest-running traditional publishing house. What better way to celebrate these literary milestones than publishing a collection of stories inspired by the Island's (and one of Canada's) most beloved author?

We certainly think the combination is a match made in publishing heaven. But it wouldn't be possible without Acorn Press's publisher and owner, Terrilee Bulger, an Island girl herself. We're also grateful for the support of publicist Karen McMullin for her efforts to spread the word far and wide about this project.

We are honoured to have helped *The ANNEthology* come to life, and hope that this collection becomes a must-have for every *Anne of Green Gables* fan.

Ready for the adventure of a lifetime? Then turn the page and get reading, Kindreds.

~ Judith and Robin

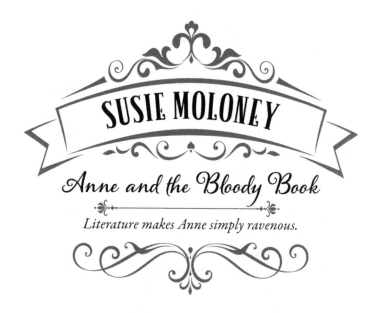

SUSIE MOLONEY

Anne and the Bloody Book

Literature makes Anne simply ravenous.

For Auntie Joannie, record player,
maker of sundaes, best playmate ever.

*T*hey could barely see the peddler behind the enormous cart coming up the road. When they did see her, Anne imagined her to be a witch.

She was short and squat with rounded shoulders that gave the impression that she had a hump on her back. But her voice was kindly, like an old grandmother's.

"Hello girls, such pretty girls, do you have some interest in ribbons and lace? I have some very pretty things," the peddler said. Diana oooohed and clapped her hands.

"Yes please!" she said.

Anne smiled indulgently and looked around for something more interesting that might be on the cart.

It was piled high with all manner of things. A dozen or so kerosene lamps hung from hooks the length of the cart. The pretty, delicate items, like ribbons, laces, and dress fabric were at the back, safe from the dusty roads, with a few slightly worn dresses, but nothing with a decent puffed sleeve. Empty milk cans, watering cans, and peach cans, lined the middle of the cart, along with all kinds of bags and travel cases and trunks, with worn edges from long years of duty before ending up on this peddler's cart.

Anne poked her fingers through a tin birdcage that surely had housed a dodo bird, so old was its paint and hinges. The cage was interesting enough, but she was more curious at what might lie underneath. When Anne moved the cage and dug further, she saw what she'd been looking for.

Books! A pile of them, under the birdcage, a wool coat, and a cigar box from Cuba, with initials carved inexpertly into the top: *LR*.

"You have books—are they on special subjects?" Anne turned to look at the peddler and Diana, who was now positively draped in ribbons and lace.

"Don't know," said the peddler, smiling. She was missing several teeth. "Can't read."

"Do you mind much if I dig them out?" Anne pulled the top book out of the pile.

The peddler waved her off and went back to weaving a particularly dingy blue velvet ribbon through Diana's jet-black hair.

(Anne allowed herself a moment of romantic envy for the nearly surreal contrast between the ribbon—however shabby—and Diana's raven tresses, but only a moment.)

There were several ornithology books, including *The Study of Birds*, but they were a shade too fact-based for Anne's taste. She preferred to think of birds as having full lives, which were invisible to most people who merely saw them as feathered garden creatures. Anne liked to believe that inside a bird's treehouse was a tiny, delicate tea set, and soft, cozy beds made up of fluffy white feathers pulled

from the bird's own down. She passed on the bird books.

She turned her attention to a children's book full of whimsical drawings of fat round bears in colourful clothing and hats with holes for their ears to poke through. Flipping to the end of the story, Anne saw a bear boy and a bear girl getting married, the bride in lacy white and the groom in a tall stovepipe hat. It was very romantic. For bears.

She pushed aside a half dozen more books until only one book remained. A distinctly mysterious book, with a black cloth cover, worn at the corners. Its spine had been opened and closed and bent so often, Anne could not read the title—it was illegible. The cover of the book was completely blank, as if there had never been a title printed there.

She opened the book to the title page.

"*A Ladie's Dark Compendium*," she read aloud. She called over to the peddler. "What a mysterious book..."

The peddler turned away from Diana—to whom she believed she had just sold the red velvet ribbon—to look at Anne. A book sale was always welcome. Then she saw the book Anne was holding.

The peddler's face went dark, but her eyes lit up. She shoved the red velvet ribbon at Diana with barely a by-your-leave, just an, "Enjoy these, Dearie."

"Do you know what you hold there, young Miss?" The peddler's voice had changed from the high-pitched, agreeable tone she'd used with Diana, to something in a lower register that implied *gravitas*—a word Anne had

only just recently learned while reading an opinion piece in *The Times*, which was the newspaper Matthew read. So she read it too.

"A very old book?" Anne answered.

"Aye. It's old all right. Older than anything you can imagine." The peddler paused and stared directly into Anne's wide eyes.

"I have a very good imagination," Anne whispered.

"Can you imagine a hundred years?"

Anne nodded. The peddler smiled.

"A thousand years?" The peddler kept smiling at Anne, who was giving the matter careful thought.

"Yes. In time, I could count to a thousand," she decided.

The peddler chuckled and tapped the side of her head. "Inside your mind, can you contemplate a million years? Years before time?"

Anne's eyes widened, now slightly frightened by the peddler's tone and intensity. The woman had gotten quite close. Anne shook her head, *no*. It was partially true—she wasn't sure she could *picture* a million years, but she could *imagine* it.

"This is a book that's seen more than that. A book of ages."

The peddler looked Anne up and down, taking her time with it. She smiled. "I think you're just the girl. I'm always right, too. I think it might even be your book already, like it was waiting for you."

When she said that, Anne felt it. She held the book in

9

both hands, thumbs on the cover, and they started to tingle. Her thumbs, then her hands, then up her arms. It thrilled for a moment and then stopped.

Suddenly, Anne had to have the ancient book.

"How much is it? I only have a nickel and I'm supposed to save it for church."

Diana came then, holding up two ribbons. "I think I'm going to get the blue one for me and the pink for Minnie May, for her Sunday dress. What do you think, Anne?"

Anne and the peddler turned together as if on some sort of dual swivel. Anne blinked at the two ribbons.

"You're a very good sister to get something for Minnie May," she said.

Diana sighed dramatically. "If I don't get her something, she'll tell Mother we spoke to a peddler."

The peddler raised her eyebrows. Diana was mortified. "I'm so sorry. I didn't mean it."

The peddler laughed. It started off small but grew to a roar.

Coughing, she turned to Anne and tapped her bony finger to Anne's chest. "I've never been wrong. The book is yours until you pass on. Be wise!"

And then she swung her cloak around her as she spun, and for a moment Anne was deliciously afraid and thought maybe—oh maybe—the peddler was going to disappear in a cloud of smoke. But instead, the woman grabbed the handles of the cart and pushed away, still cackling, in the opposite direction.

"That was nice of her," Diana said, smiling. "What

kind of book is it?" She'd draped the ribbons over her wrist so they wouldn't get wrinkled. Naturally, she'd picked the nicest ones—neither of these were dingy or dirty. Diana admired how they hung brightly against the sleeve of her dress.

"I don't know," Anne said. "She was very odd about it." Her right hand clutched her throat and her face got a faraway look. "She kept saying I was the girl to have the book, and that she was always right. It was very mysterious." Anne took a breath. "I almost felt as if I were in a trance when she spoke to me."

Diana's eyes widened and her voice dropped. "A trance. Like at the fair?"

Neither of them were supposed to go to any of the tent shows at the spring fair, but Anne had talked Diana into going. As soon as they saw a banner with the spinning, mesmerizing eyes for Dr. Hypnoso, they could not miss his show. He was a loud man with greasy black hair and a thin mustache. He shouted for volunteers, and Mr. Armory, who worked at the mill, put his hand up. Everyone laughed when he said he wanted the hypnotizer to scare the demon drink out of him. But the hypnotizer made Mr. Armory moo like a cow, on all fours.

"Not like that. More like she held me *rapt* as if I could hear no voice but hers. All around me, the world had disappeared." Anne was quite proud of the description.

Diana grabbed her friend's hand, "Promise me you'll not be a cow, Anne! Promise me now!"

So Anne promised, and the two of them broke into a

11

run, at first because they had emotions they needed to outrun, but then just because it was a beautiful autumnal day, and the air smelled like apples, and they were both very fast.

And they ran and ran all the way to the Barry place, just because.

Later, after prayers and after she heard the springs in Marilla's bed creak as she lay down for the night, Anne relit her lantern.

She felt around under her mattress until the frayed corner of the book brushed her fingertips. She reached further and pulled out the book, carefully, carefully, so as not to scratch or mar the worn and ancient cloth just barely clinging to the pressed binding.

Anne drew the candle close, opening the book on the bed (not far from where she said her prayers), and read the first page, just after the flyleaf. It was in Latin and her Latin was rough, but it translated to:

"Mourn the Past, Attend the Present, Rule the Future"

The phrasing touched Anne's philosopher's soul, and she leaned back on her bed, her scrawny shoulders pressing into the brass headboard. She put a hand to her heart and repeated the phrase twice more and finally admitted that she didn't think she'd ever heard such a perfect piece of advice.

"Mourn the Past, Attend the Present, Rule the Future"

She turned to the first page with equal parts reluctance and an incendiary excitement that she had never felt before, at least not since six Tuesdays ago when she and

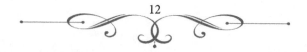

Diana had gone with Miss Stacy to the bookstore in Charlottetown. Anne had been so filled with anticipation that her body literally trembled when they went inside. A whole *shop* full of books! Books that could be hers!

She'd bought a novel and a book on deportment. She'd wanted very much to buy a penny dreadful as they were called, but both Miss Stacy and Diana were so scandalized that Anne gave up on that particular dream.

(The cover featured a heaving, bosomed girl hiding just around a corner from only the shadow of a man silhouetted in a golden circle of light thrown by a streetlamp— Miss Stacy gasped and Diana's cheeks went a brilliant red.)

Anne turned the page with *that* feeling.

The first word of the book was "IF," gloriously illuminated in gold leaf.

"If you have opened this book, you may already be doomed. From here you read of your own volition and partake in the damning of your own soul. The pages of this book tell the unwholesome history of the unseen world. You will learn the ways of darkness.

Stop now, or be forever lost."

Anne paused, her finger poised over the upper corner of the page for a moment, utterly still, her eyes wide.

"Wondrous. Utterly wondrous," she said, and after just only the merest, tiniest reluctance.

She turned the page.

Anne read late into the night and into the morning, her head filling with the most exotic knowledge,

bewitched in such a way that she eventually read inde-
pendently of her mind, her body, or her memory. She just
read. She was the words. She was the page. She was the
book.

Anne was bleary-eyed the next morning at breakfast
and Marilla noticed. She put Anne's oatmeal down in
front of the girl, and then her milk, and finally a wedge of
cheese and a slice of bread, and sat herself back down at
the table to finish her own tea. Anne, meanwhile, sat
practically swaying in her seat.

"Anne *Shirley*," Marilla said, trying to keep the annoyed
edge out of her voice. "I've made you breakfast and now
you must eat it. You'll not go to school on an empty
stomach from this house."

She sipped her tea.

Anne's head had been bent this whole time, eyes either
closed or fixed on the floor, Marilla couldn't tell. But now
Anne lifted her head, with slow deliberation, inch by inch
until she stared at Marilla with eyes red-rimmed from a
lack of sleep. When Anne spoke, her voice was thick.

"Meat," she rasped. "I need meat." She pushed the
bowl away and stood. Without looking back, she left the
house, leaving Marilla staring at Anne, her mouth
opening and closing like a surprised fish.

"For heaven's sakes! There's roast beef in your sandwich," Marilla said, rising. She shook her head angrily,
watching the girl walking away. "*Anne*! Anne Shirley, you
come back here—" she called and called, but the girl just
grew smaller in the window.

Anne walked quickly, her stride broad and unladylike. She tore open the brown paper bag with her lunch and grabbed at the sandwich, letting the piece of pie made with this year's apples fall to the ground, along with the napkin and fork Marilla had packed for her.

Anne pulled the bread off the sandwich and let it fall, too. She shoved the beefy contents into her mouth until it was overstuffed. She chewed like she walked, with huge bites. Spittle formed on the sides of her mouth. She swallowed large chunks of the meat, her throat opening to accept them, her belly hungrily receiving them. Her eyes nearly rolled back inside her head with ecstasy, so delicious was the meat, so finely textured the fibrous nature of it, so apparent the taste of something primal and earthy.

There was no one to hear, but at one point, she growled.

When the meat was gone, when Anne could finally think a clear thought again, she dropped to the sitting rock by the school shortcut and tried to untangle her thoughts.

There were *so* many.

The inside of her head was like a beehive. It went *buzz buzz buzz*. And she could almost feel the stings.

What do I know, now?

What has become of me?

Anne held her head in her hands and tried to remember the book, reading it, learning its secrets.

Oh, the secrets.

It began in a time before history, when the earth was

just vibrations and the ebb and flow of the oceans. It spoke of the Early Ones harnessing that power.

And she was different now.

Anne became ardently aware of the world around her: the feel of solid rock beneath her, the canopy of trees over her. Every sense was heightened. She could smell all of the forest, although certain scents stood out frightfully clearly.

She could smell prey. She could hear their tiny hearts thundering behind their finely boned ribs. She could smell their fear as they scurried from nest to food to nest again. The predators were there too, their noses in the air, ever aware of the vulnerable and delicious food around them.

Something snapped its jaws and Anne could smell the blood of victory.

She was drooling. She swiped her sleeve against her chin and stood to go, listening to the snap of teeth, the crack of bones, the burst of organs, the feast that happened somewhere beyond where she could see, in that very forest.

"Anne!" Diana's voice floated sweetly from above. Anne looked up with an almost feral antagonism to see her friend skipping toward her. She chewed and swallowed what was left in her mouth, a tiny bit of the shredded meat clinging to her lip.

Nearly out of breath as she drew near, Diana gasped prettily before grabbing Anne's hands in both of her own.

"Your hands are so cold! Are you sick?" Diana fretted.

Anne smiled—like her old self—and got to her feet.

"Everything is fine. I'm just right."

Diana sighed with relief. "Minnie May liked her ribbon and hasn't said a thing yet, but I'm so afraid she'll tell. Mother will be so angry. I don't dare try to think of a lie—"

Anne stared blankly at Diana for a long moment, her eyes unfocused and still rimmed with red from a lack of sleep. She stared a great deal longer than seemed normal without blinking. Diana shook her friend's shoulder, delicately, as they emerged from the woods, with the school up ahead.

"You're scaring me," Diana whispered. She looked helplessly over at the children on the playground. The boys kicked a ball around, and the girls hovered around Josie Pye, who had a new pair of boots from Charlotte-town.

"Anne!"

Anne snapped out of it. She blinked a few times to get the cobwebs out and finally managed, "Diana."

"What's wrong with you?"

One drags the gutter upwards from belly to sternum, not the other way; the other way is to kill the host, when what is desired is the intestines to fall to the—

"I stayed up too late. Reading."

Oh, I won't tell you the best *part about the book, my darling Diana, my bosom friend, for you would crumble in tears and maybe you would even bring up your breakfast if I told you about a book that taught me such a secret—*

"Reading your new book! Of course! That is so fun. Is

it a novel? Is it a love story? I love a secret love..." Diana's voice faded. It was all right though, because she was talking about the same old things. Anne knew them by heart.

—such secrets I've been taught. I don't dare tell you that if you say the right words when you consume something—that means eat it up—*the essence of that thing becomes yours.*

For instance, darling Diana, if I ate Minnie May, I would be able to cry and moan and whine until someone ate me *up.*

The thought of eating Minnie May made Anne salivate. And then her face twisted in disgust at the images in her own mind. She struggled to come back out of her head. Diana was still talking.

"...even though I know Minnie May will spoil it eventually. What do you think—" Diana tilted her head to better show off the brilliant baby blue velvet ribbon woven through her hair. "When Mother asked where it came from, I said, *this old thing?*" Her mouth opened wide with the delight of the lie. But then she corrected herself. "It's not exactly a lie. The ribbon *is* old. Not new, for certain. Isn't that right?" She waited for Anne to answer. Instead, Anne tangled her fingers in Diana's sooty tresses.

"So beautiful," she mumbled.

Diana frowned, confused, and instinctively pulled away. She opened her mouth to say something—

But then the school bell rang and everyone raced to the door, Anne lastly, moving slowly and with a strange determination. A narrow-eyed Josie Pye watched her because Josie Pye was always on the lookout for something she didn't already know.

At lunch, Anne had nothing to eat. But she shook her head (and maybe snarled) at the biscuit Diana offered her. It was not meat.

"You're acting awfully strange today, Anne," Diana sniffed. "I hope you're not angry with me. Tell me if you are?" When Anne's eyes fell on her, they looked feverish, and Diana was taken aback once more. Without even realizing it, she recoiled slightly.

"Please say you're alright," she whispered. "You're my bosom friend."

But Anne's eyes had now moved to the sports field where Gilbert Blythe had control of the ball. He moved like a dancer, every muscle taut and working. His fine arms spread wide to keep balance, his long calves pressing against the fabric of his trousers. She ran her tongue over her lips. She could hear his voice inside her head.

Carrots.

Using all her focus, she directed her laser gaze on a spot between Gilbert's broad shoulders. She muttered new words—

Mea sunt

Mea sunt

—in her head, her lips moving without sound.

Mine.

Gilbert's kick went wild, and he stopped, suddenly spinning around and looking for the source of whatever distracted him. His eyes landed on—

Carrots.

—Anne. Their eyes locked and his eyes closed lazily as if he felt suddenly sleepy. Or loving. When they opened, they were still locked on hers. He smiled, one side of his ripe red lips rising slightly higher than the other, a crooked grin. A pretty crooked grin—

Someone in the game (*kill him)* shouted Gilbert's name, and he turned away, as if a spell had broken.

Anne's lip curled in a hiss.

"Are you mad?" Diana still waited on an explanation, a reassurance. Anne sighed.

"I was an orphan, Diana. I've seen some shit." Anne muttered the last part, but Diana still heard and her eyes had gone as wide as saucers and her mouth hung agape. Anne reached out and pressed her friend's chin up to close it.

"You *are* my bosom friend," she said. "And I won't eat you."

She may not have said the last part out loud. How could she be sure?

Anne stood and wandered off in the direction of the forest. Diana called after her. "Anne! *Anne*! You can't leave school!"

Anne found a nice clearing, which at one time she would have called it *a sun-dappled dale, protected by kindly tall soldiers of wood and greenery, a haven for the imagination and woodland creatures to commune.* Now, however, she saw a turned-over log and plopped down on it, knowing no one could see where she was. Not from the

path. Not unless they came close. And if they did—

What would I do?

She thought now the question may be *what CAN I do?* Because inside her, she could feel a softness in her belly, where her boundaries once lay. Now they were sagging and soft and could be broken through at a moment's notice. No. Not a moment's *notice.* A moment's scent.

She breathed in the air around her, deeply, savouring the myriad of smells, the dank earth, the wet, muggy air, the rotting underbrush.

Time went.

Anne's body slumped, legs open, elbows on her knees. Her head sagged on her neck, heavy with new knowledge. Her eyes were still red. Her body felt like an entity of its own. And without bidding, air filled her lungs and she—

"*Obsecro tenebras pro meis necessitatibus et cupiditatibus,*" she intoned. Her eyes stared straight ahead. A small mole or vole or such scurried in the underbrush, away from her, terrified. She did not reach down and snatch the creature. She had other things in mind.

Her body seized, her breath heaved raggedly, her eyes sunk farther back in her head. Images from her life rolled over and over inside her mind like a nickelodeon.

I saw a nickelodeon at the fair—

meat meat meat

Twins. The orphanage. Mr. Thomas and his well-deserved death. The Hammonds, all of them. Matthew. Marilla. They swirled around in Anne's head, so fast, their faces blurred, and her stomach growled with a great need

21

and—

"Anne!" Anne snapped back, literally, her neck making a terribly, almost fatal, cracking sound, her eyes wild, the words still on her tongue—

"Anne!" Diana battled through the brush at a clip, for her, considering her skirts and button-up boots. "I've been looking for you since school was over! I was so worried—"

But Anne heard none of these sounds. What Anne's fevered brain picked up was something quite different. A series of high-pitched squeals that accompanied hot, sweet breath, a fast-beating heart, full of blood and youth and vitality.

jabber jabbber jabbbbberrrrferdin booo ca ca ca bleda

Anne stood and shouted, "Jabber jabbber jabbbberrr-ferdin booo ca ca ca—" and Diana staggered backwards, falling as if punched. She stared up at her friend, her lips twisted in a confused, uncertain smile as if to think, *This is a tease, isn't it, Anne—*

She barely got her last word out.

"Ann—"

Anne loomed over her, arms raised. *"WITH AN 'E,' DIANA!"*

And with that, Anne dropped to her knees beside Diana, knowing that if nothing else, her friend would want her to find sustenance, should she need to. And Diana, bosom friend that she was, would be happy to be that sustenance. Anne buried her head in the soft flesh of Diana's shoulder and bit down.

It was true then.

Sugar and spice and everything nice.

Anne fed.

She exhausted herself. Bloated and full, she fell back onto the rich forest floor. Her stomach rolled its contents around, attacking them from every side, rolling rolling, becoming a part of her. Becoming her.

It was exhausting. Anne's eyes closed.

"*Obsecro tenebras pro meis necessitatibus et cupiditatibus.*" Later, she woke, shrieking. Her body, as if on its own mechanics, lurched upward, and she stood, taller she believed, than she had been. As she did, she raised her hands and pulled out the braids that she'd put in that morning. She tugged at the plain brown ribbons until they fell to the forest floor. She laced her fingers into the plaits and pulled until they loosened.

"*Pro meis necessitatibus.*" The sky darkened as if awaiting an ominous sign from higher yet. Distantly, there was a low rumble that had nothing to do with rain. The air crackled. A half dozen sparrows burst out of the tree closest to her, with a collective shriek of fear.

Anne neither saw nor heard any of this. She stroked her now loose hair. And she repeated the phrase two more times like the book said:

"*Pro meis necessitatibus.*"

"*Pro meis necessitatibus.*"

The sky cleared eventually. Whatever birds had left slowly returned. The clearing settled.

She rested. It was pleasant in the dale. There was decay under the covering shrubs. The smell of feces and old

bones, and dripping fluids of dead animals. The wasting of vegetation, the ouroboros of life-death-life-death, each feeding on the other. It was peaceful.

Somewhere deep inside Anne, there was a yearning. A mourning. A cry that went unanswered. She may even have heard it, but just ignored it.

"*Obsecro tenebras pro meis necessitatibus et cupiditatibus.*"

I ask darkness for my needs and desires.

She said it again, but with a sing-song voice in a tune that reminded her of another darkness.

Under her breath she sang, "*Ring around the rosie, a pocket full of posies...*"

And part of her felt like she remembered that. The black death.

Hush-a, hush-a, we all fall down!

It felt complete. Even as she imagined a group of children dancing in a circle, while plague victims dropped to cobblestones.

Anne sighed and wished for a mirror.

The air was chilly when she rose, and she wrapped her shawl over her head and hugged it close. It was near dark when she got back to Green Gables, but lights burned through the windows. There was a carriage in the yard that wasn't theirs, and Anne could see Rachel Lynde peering out into the night from Marilla's kitchen.

They must have heard her coming because there was a shout and the front door flew open. It was Matthew first, surprisingly quick on his feet for a man of his age, and

24

then Marilla, with Mr. Barry and Rachel Lynde following behind.

"Anne! Anne!" Marilla shouted. As for Matthew, he just slowed his step, but never quit Anne's direction. He smiled more and more broadly as he got closer. Once he was close enough to touch, he took both her hands in his. "I was worried about you," he said.

She smiled because she knew she ought to. And Matthew was a benign soul. After him came Marilla, at more of a clip and far less stoic.

"By wrath, Anne! Where have you been! You've had us worried to tears!" She sounded sad, but her expression was fierce. Under the ferocity, Anne could see the sincere concern. She could see everything. She had many eyes now.

"I'm sorry," she said, graciously. "I lost track of time." Her brain scanned her many thoughts, dreams, imaginations until she found a suitable one. "I found a magical place, with dappling sunlight, and later, burning orange from the sunset. The moon shone right through the trees where I reposed, and it was truly a majestic and magical place. I got lost in my thoughts—" Anne allowed her eyes to tear up responsibly. "I'm sorry if I worried you," she said.

"Just come inside," Marilla said, taking charge of the girl's arm in hers and leading her to the house.

"We expected to find Diana with you—wasn't she with you?" Mr. Barry asked, his forehead a collection of lines. Anne could feel his fear, his concern. His brain rolled

around too fast. Anne was too tired to keep up. She was too sad.

She both knew and didn't know what happened.

"She wasn't, Mr. Barry," Anne said, in her old voice.

"Well," he said, face scrunched up with worry. "Where is she then? She didn't come home and isn't at school—"

Anne's eyes half-closed in remembrance—

She's right here, Mr. Barry. Right here in my belly, where she's forever the prettiest one, forever the tastiest—

She was caught. They all stared. *That* had to stop.

"Wherever she was, I'm sure she is safe at home by now." With a last sly look at the chorus of grown faces around her, Anne swooned.

(Old Anne would have been so proud.)

And they swarmed, catching her, petting her, soothing her. Matthew carried her into the house and sat her on the bench. Clinging to the hope that Anne had given him, Mr. Barry bid everyone good night and set out to see if his daughter was at home. Hoping she was at home.

"My goodness, child, you will run rings around the people who care about you," Rachel Lynde said, tsk-tsking at the end. It was all Anne could do to keep from spinning her head and *hissing* at her. It surprised her, the urge. To distract herself, she dropped her shawl and shook the leaves and debris of the forest from it.

Marilla's shocked expression and scream made everyone jump.

"*What's happened to your hair?!*"

It was jet-black. Ebony. Night sky. The sooty raven

black of goddesses from ancient Egypt, the deepest, darkest onyx. It was extraordinary, and Anne's heart leapt with joy and gratitude.

Marilla's did not.

The older woman ranted and raged against Anne's silliness, against the peddler she assumed Anne got some hair-dyeing concoction from, wasting good money on vanity.

"How are you going to explain this, Anne?" Marilla said, her ire expired, replaced by true confusion and concern. She put her hand gently on Anne's hair and shook her head. "What you've always wanted."

Marilla excused herself, reminding Anne to say her prayers and get into bed. What a worrisome night. They were all exhausted.

Anne's smile broadened. It was a *wonderful* night. She looked back to the mirror and admired it. Her complexion was fairer somehow, against it. Her freckles hardly noticeable.

What will Gilbert think?

She knew without using her imagination what Gilbert would think. Gilbert would love her new hair. She wished she could show Diana. But she couldn't. Not now. Not ever. A pang unusual to this remarkable day, the one thing she hadn't felt, in the melee of feelings that she had managed to have: sadness.

Bosom friends.

Eventually, everyone would come around once she looked them in the eye. Looked through them. Looked

into them.

Anne hummed and busied herself with changing for the night. She put on her nightdress and brushed her hair one hundred strokes until it caught the gleam of the moon and shone like polished tourmaline. She crawled under the covers, feeling the hard flatness of the book under her mattress. The book made her feel safe. And strong. So strong.

The book on the table beside her bed was a romantic story about a girl and a boy who went to sea. She'd liked it well enough. . .before. She opened it, but could not focus.

She personally would take on the responsibility of helping to raise Minnie May to be a sister Diana would be proud to have. She'd always suspected a bosom friend might be in Minnie May.

Maybe she'll taste like her sister.

Anne pushed that away, far away, down low where the rest of the evil was resting and waiting. She'd deal with it tomorrow.

Tomorrow, she would talk to Gilbert. Not tease him, not to challenge him. Just talk to him—softly—like a girl would. She would smile and he would smile back. He will be her beau.

She was going to get a beautiful dress with puffed sleeves. There were going to be a lot of puffed sleeves.

Anne wondered if Josie Pye tasted like cornmeal.

She decided she was too tired to read after all. Before she closed the book on her lap, she reached for a pretty blue ribbon to hold her place. Was that a spot of some-

thing on it? She held it close to her face and examined it. A little red-brown spot.

She licked it.

Uh huh.

She put it in the gutter of the book and closed it, putting it back on the nightstand. A full, delicious breeze blew in from the woods through her window.

Things were going to change in Avonlea.

So much already had.

Susie Moloney is the author of *Bastion Falls*, *A Dry Spell*, *The Dwelling*, *The Thirteen*, and *Things Withered*. Her books have sold in 18 countries and have been translated into 12 languages. She also writes for film and television. She often collaborates with her partner, playwright Vern Thiessen, as well as her dog, Scrappy, who is full of ideas.

HOPE DALVAY

In Search of Kindred Spirits

The search begins in the scariest of places...junior high.

Thank you to all the kindred spirits I've ever met. You've lifted me up when I've been down, always appearing at just the right time, and often in the unlikeliest of places: on the school bus (helping Anxious Me find a seat), in the hallway before a test (reassuring Stressed-Out Me that I've got this), and on the other side of my dorm room wall (letting Homesick Me know that I'm not alone). Whether you're a relative or a friend, or whether we've met in person or online, you've all become my family.

Ms. Stacy placed a sheet of lined paper and a pen on my desk. "I would like an accurate, detailed account of what happened in the cafeteria today, please."

"Is this *really* necessary?" asked Wretched Boy, who was sitting across the aisle. "Everybody knows what happened. It's not exactly a mystery." He used his pen to push the paper away from him, as though it were toxic.

Not me.

"I'd be happy to, Ms. Stacy, since I find writing to be such a cathartic exercise." I stole a glance at Wretched Boy, who looked confused. Dolt. I would be magnanimous. "The word 'cathartic' is defined as—"

"I know what it means," interrupted Wretched Boy. He retrieved the sheet from the edge of his desk and started to write.

So did I. And it would be good. Ms. Stacy would believe my account. I shall call it:

"Chaos in the Cafeteria"

"Blythe, come sit with us!" called Ruby Gillis, fluttering her hand invitingly. "We want to hear all about your trip." She then flashed her trademark magnetic smile.

The boy pivoted on his heels, pulled by an invisible force to our table.

Blythe. Hmm…what an interesting name, I thought. *Happy, lighthearted in meaning. I wonder if it suits him.*

"Blythe, there's a free seat beside me!" announced Josie Pye, flipping her hair so it fell forward over her shoulders.

Without hesitation, Blythe slid into the empty seat beside me. Either he had failed to hear Josie, or he had chosen to ignore her. I was thinking it was the latter. Josie had spoken quite clearly, even patting the chair beside hers. She then shot me an annoyed glance, her lip curled in disdain.

Breaking news: Josie Pye is ticked off at me. Again.

But why? She barely knows me. I'm still the new kid at school, after all. Maybe…it's not personal. Maybe…it's business. You see, my adoptive parent runs a bake shop. The Bend in the Road Bakery—isn't that a delicious name? I thought of it myself. You know the place? Most folks around here think of it as "Marilla's bakery." Apparently, it takes time for a new name to catch on. Sigh. Anyway, back to my business theory—Josie's family runs Pyes' Fries. (Why the Pyes don't sell pies from their food truck is beyond me. It just seems like a no-brainer.) I'm not sure why Josie would feel threatened. I'm sure Avonlea and the surrounding communities can support both a food truck and a bakery. But I digress.

"Oh, hi, I'm Anne. That's Anne with an 'e,'" I said, by way of introduction. I always make a point of spelling out my name when I meet someone for the first time. "Ann"

without an "e" looks so dreadfully dull. Adding an "e" really gives it an extra oomph, in my humble opinion.

"Nice to meet you, *Annie,*" said Blythe.

Did he purposely mispronounce my name? I wondered. However, before I could politely correct him, I was distracted by a tap on my arm. I leaned to my right to catch what Jane Andrews was saying. Jane always speaks in a whisper. I haven't figured out why, though. Is she incredibly shy, or is she physically unable to raise her voice? Or…is it her way of drawing people in? Hmm… maybe quiet Jane has hidden depths. I should give this some more thought.

Anyway, my attention was *literally* pulled away from Jane's opinion on the state of today's education. (I'm kidding; she was just complaining about how much homework we had.) Blythe yanked one of my braids, causing me to turn in his direction. He then uttered the most insulting thing imaginable. And I quote, "Carrots! Carrots!" And no, he was *not* referring to today's cafeteria offering.

It was my hair. The bane of my existence.

My greatest wish—nay, my *second* greatest wish—is for my hair to be any colour other than red. My greatest wish, of course, is for world peace.

Obviously, Blythe hurt my feelings ex-cru-ci-at-ing-ly. Henceforth, he shall be "Wretched Boy" in our shared existence. Naturally, there was little else to do but grab my lunch tray and hit Wretched Boy over the head with it. For a moment…

I raised my hand. "Oh, Ms. Stacy, could I have more paper, please?"

Wretched Boy then raised his hand and also asked for another sheet. I stared at him in disbelief. *Why is Wretched Boy waggling his eyebrows at me? Does he seriously think he's going to win this writing duel? Nuh-uh. Little does he know that I'm even better at wielding a pen than a lunch tray.* I returned my attention to my essay, doubling down on the details.

...I was exhilarated. It felt empowering to stand up to a bully. However, a teeny-tiny sliver of regret soon sliced into my soul. As a proponent of world peace, I felt conflicted. Perhaps resorting to violence as my first option was not appropriate. Luckily for Wretched Boy, I hadn't ordered ketchup with my fries.

"Food fight!" yelled someone.

Chaos ensued. Half-eaten food flew through the air. Some kids dove for cover under the tables, while others threw themselves into the fray. It wasn't a food fight—it was an all-out war.

"Okay, time's up," announced Ms. Stacy. "Please exchange your papers and read them carefully. I think this is the best way to see the situation from someone else's perspective. If you agree with the other person's account, please sign your name at the bottom of the page. If not, we will have to discuss the matter more thoroughly, together."

Wretched Boy leaned across the aisle so we could make the exchange. I had tremendous respect for Ms. Stacy. I'd moved a lot as a former foster kid and attended many schools. And she was the kindest guidance counsellor I'd ever met. However, this "see the situation from someone else's perspective" idea of hers was making me question her judgment.

Okay, Wretched Boy, what do you have to say for yourself? I started in on his account:

> I, Gilbert Blythe, teased Anne (spelled with an "e") by pulling her braid and referring to her hair as "carrots." She reacted—some might even say "overreacted"—by bouncing her lunch tray off my head. A food fight, in which neither of us participated, erupted in the cafeteria. I humbly apologize for my actions.

A few things immediately jumped out at me. One: Wretched Boy's account was brief and matter-of-fact. Two: Wretched Boy had covered the remainder of his sheets of paper with doodles of stick figures engaged in an epic food fight. Three: Wretched Boy's first name was "Gilbert." It sounded even more old-fashioned than my name. No wonder he went by "Blythe," instead.

Hmm…how DO you persuade others to call you by a different name, anyway? Oh, how I'd love to be called "Cordelia." With a name like that, I'd be destined for greatness.

Ms. Stacy politely cleared her throat. With a sigh, I

signed my name. I couldn't argue with the facts as stated. At Ms. Stacy's urging, Wretched Boy and I exchanged papers once again for final approval before submitting them. The only change he had made to my account involved crossing out each mention of "Wretched Boy" and replacing it with "Gilbert Blythe." Okay, okay, so he had a name—duly noted. And as someone who's a believer in the power of names, I will honour his wishes... even if he's still my sworn enemy. I will also give him credit for decent penmanship.

"Now that the truth has been revealed, it's time for the consequences," said Ms. Stacy. "Please report to the janitor in the cafeteria. He'll explain how he wants you to clean up the mess."

"But we weren't involved in the food fight," grumbled Blythe.

"It's not our fault!" I protested.

"But isn't it?" Ms. Stacy tilted her head. "As soon as you finish there, go to your final class of the day." She paused to study her computer screen. "I believe you both have art."

With my back ramrod straight, I marched from Ms. Stacy's office to the cafeteria. Gilbert Blythe fell into step beside me, occasionally saying, "Anne, Anne with an 'e,'" in a desperate attempt to get my attention. I ignored him.

When we arrived in the cafeteria, the janitor handed each of us a bucket of soapy water and some sponges. I immediately set about dislodging a slice of pizza stuck cheese-side down from a metal chair.

"So...you're giving me the silent treatment," observed Blythe. "How original of you. Well, I shall do the opposite." And that's exactly what he did. He blathered on and on for the duration of the cleanup. He began by lampooning the teachers of Carmody Consolidated School and then shifted his focus to our fellow classmates. I tried ignoring him, but his impersonations were comically accurate. He then moved on to describing the splatter marks and stains on the walls and tables in detail, presumably because he had run out of school gossip. Or perhaps it was his way of annoying me. At one point, he claimed to have found a splatter that resembled Mr. Phillips, the art teacher. I was tempted to drop everything and see it for myself.

No, it's a trap! Stay strong. You've got this. Yet...I wonder how accurate the splatter of Mr. Phillips really is. Does it include his wispy combover? Just one little look-see...

Fortunately, the janitor told us we were done before I compromised my morals. I bolted from the cafeteria, with Gilbert Blythe striding quickly to keep pace. There was just enough time to make an appearance in art class before the dismissal bell rang. To my dismay, only two seats were available. I slipped into one of them; Blythe slid into the other.

"Well, well, well, if it isn't the food-fight instigators," said Mr. Phillips, giving each of us a handout. "I've just finished informing the class about this semester's major assignment. I'm calling it 'The Passion Project.' Basically, express what you're passionate about through art."

Ooh, I have so many passions. The hard part will be narrowing the list to just one. I wonder if Mr. Phillips would accept an essay. The written word is an art form, isn't it?

Mr. Phillips continued, "For this project, the forms of art are limited to illustration, sculpture, or film. The rest of the class has already partnered up so that leaves the two of you"—he pointed a stubby, paint-stained finger at Blythe and me—"to work together."

"So, Anne with an 'e,'" whispered Blythe, "it looks like you're going to have to speak to me, after all. Feel free to start anytime. Still no response. Okay, I have a confession. I can't draw—well, except for stick figures. But you already know that. Please tell me you can draw or sculpt."

I shook my head.

"Filmmaking it is. Okay, I'll give you my email and cell number in case you ever feel like communicating." He then scribbled his info on my handout.

"Oh, I have an idea."

"She's speaking to me! You have an idea? That's awesome. Well, what is it?"

"I think we should work separately."

The dismissal bell rang, and I fled the scene.

Waves of relief washed over me as I staggered off the school bus. I strolled up the dusty lane, each step bringing me closer to *home*. Oh, how I loved that word! Home was where I felt safe…and loved…and understood. For the first twelve years of my life, I didn't have a home—well, not in my strict definition of the word. I had grown up in foster care, moving from family to family. Some were welcoming and caring, others not so much. Then, a few months ago, my life changed drastically…for the better. I was adopted by Matthew and Marilla Cuthbert, an elderly brother and sister who owned a small farm called Green Gables. I couldn't believe it—me, a city girl, living on a farm and surrounded by nature and all its wondrous delights.

HONK, HONK, HONK. HISS, HISSSSS…One wondrous delight I could do without, however, was the flock of geese guarding the property. With their necks lowered to the ground, they waddled with alarming speed toward me. I shifted from a stroll to a sprint. With a mighty leap, I landed on the sandstone step. My cherished ritual of pausing to pinch myself at the entrance of Green Gables would have to be abandoned for today, what with those vicious geese hot on my heels. Plus, I didn't want to keep my best friend waiting.

Mindful of Marilla's spotless floors, I kicked off my shoes. All was quiet: Marilla was at the bakery, and Matthew was working in a back field. I dashed upstairs to my sanctuary. Oh, how I loved my little white room. I'd never had a space to call my own before arriving at Green Gables. Marilla shakes her head at my decorating style, and says that flowers and leaves and seashells belong in the great outdoors. But I respectfully disagree.

I plopped down on the wicker chair and gazed out my

window at the mansion looming in the distance. I'd overheard Marilla lament to herself how it was a sad, sad day when the Orchard Slope farmhouse was torn down and replaced with that monstrosity. The neighbouring house was indeed lacking in charm. However, I'd never admit this to my dearest friend in the world, who just so happened to spend her summers in the said monstrosity.

My cell buzzed: an incoming FaceTime call.

Decline or accept? If only all of life's questions were so easy to answer. Accept! Accept!

"Diana, you won't believe what happened today!" I couldn't wait to give my bestie the scoop.

"I already know! There's a video of it on YouTube. Oh, Anne, how could you smack Blythe on the head with your tray?" As usual, Diana was well informed on all the drama. "And the food fight…that was wild. It made me *almost* wish I went to your school instead of in town."

"How could I? Oh, I had a very, very good reason. He had the *brazenness* to refer to my hair as 'carrots'! And you know how I feel about my red hair. So I put that bully in his place."

"By resorting to violence? That doesn't sound like my peace-loving friend. Maybe…Blythe was just teasing you…with affection."

I squeaked in protest.

"Like I'm teasing you now," said Diana, grinning. "So…Blythe is back in Avonlea. Interesting."

"A bully…a tormentor…an oppressor…is back in Avonlea, and you find it…*interesting*?"

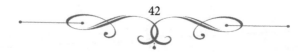

"Oh, Anne, he's the opposite of a bully. You really should forgive him."

I rolled my eyes. "A hero to the downtrodden, I'm sure."

"The down-what? Never mind. And, yeah, the fact Blythe's back in Avonlea *is* interesting."

"Not to me. The iron has entered into my soul."

Diana exhaled. "Okay, I can't let that one slide. What are you even talking about?"

"It means he has hurt me deeply, and I shall never, ever forgive him."

"That's too bad," she said, shaking her head in mock concern. "I bet Blythe has lots of stories to tell. And I know how much you love stories. You see, he's been travelling with his dad for the past two years ever since—"

"Diana! I don't hear you practising." A familiar and often unwelcome voice drifted into our conversation.

"That's my mom. I gotta go," Diana said. "I have a piano recital on Saturday."

"But that means you won't be in Avonlea this weekend! What about the paddleboarding adventure we planned for tomorrow?"

"You can still go with Josie and Ruby and Jane. Don't give me that look, Anne. It's important to make other friends. Though…I'd be wary of Josie, of course."

"Diana, you aren't talking to that—"

Call ended.

I sighed. It didn't take much of an imagination to figure out what Diana's mom was about to say. She wasn't

exactly my biggest fan.

I'd been so wrapped up in my thoughts I hadn't noticed Marilla standing in the doorway.

"So, how many stitches did the Blythe boy need?" she asked.

"You know about the…incident?"

"Of course. Ms. Stacy called to inform me. But I'd already heard the news by that time. Rachel dropped by the bakery to tell me personally. It's on The Facebook. It amazes me how Rachel, who barely knows how to turn on a computer, is a social media aficionado. So…how many stitches?"

"None. The tray bounced off his head."

Marilla nodded. "The Blythes are known to be a hardheaded lot."

Wait, did Marilla just crack a joke? Does that mean she's not angry with me?

She continued, "So, what made you do such a thing? Rachel has her theories, but I'd like to hear it from you."

"He…he called me 'carrots'—you know, because of my red hair. I was angry." I gave Marilla a careful look, trying to read her. "I'm sorry, Marilla. I really am. You aren't going to send me back to foster care, are you?"

Marilla strode across the room and then knelt beside my chair. "Anne, don't be ridiculous. That will never, ever happen." She gently squeezed my hand. "Our lives were so quiet before you came. The silence was suffocating us. You know Matthew would be lost without you. And I— well, I'd be lost without you, too."

My shoulders sagged in relief. "Though, I guess, I deserve to be punished. Maybe...I should be grounded?" I suggested. *And that way, I have an excuse for not paddleboarding tomorrow. It won't be the same without Diana.*

"That was my first thought, too," said Marilla. "But I talked it over with Rachel, and she convinced me that you need more socialization, not less. So you can go paddleboarding tomorrow, as planned. Now, be a dear and help me to my feet. I'm not as limber as I once was."

"Good morning, Rachel!" I called out as I bounded up the steps of the bookmobile. "Did you happen to catch the sunset yesterday evening? It was absolutely breathtaking. The fluffy clouds and the pink skies reminded me of cotton candy. Did you ever wonder how cotton candy got its name? I mean, I know it looks like cotton, but the thought of eating cotton makes me want to gag. I'm not too late, am I?"

"No, you've still got time, Anne. We're not scheduled to leave for another five minutes. I have the books you placed on hold. As I'm sure you're aware, you're at your borrowing limit. You seem to be going through a classic literature phase, I see. I'm more of a juicy Hollywood tell-all kind of gal myself—that is, when I can find time to read."

I bit my lip, desperate to hide my smile. The fact that Rachel Lynde worked on the bookmobile had initially confused me. She didn't seem like the bookish type at all. Marilla, however, theorized it was perfect for Rachel. What other job allowed her to travel around the local communities, chatting with folks and collecting the latest gossip?

"Ah, Gilbert, I see you're ready to check out your books. My, you've got quite a stack there," observed Rachel.

Did she say "Gilbert"? Is it possible that there's more than one Gilbert in Avonlea? I think I already know the answer to that. Oh no, that means he heard me go on and on about how the clouds reminded me of cotton candy.

"In light of yesterday's events, perhaps I should stand between you two," suggested Rachel. "I could act as a human shield for you, Gilbert."

"Anne doesn't appear armed with a lunch tray, so I think I'm safe," he said with a laugh. "Though there are plenty of books here she could thump me over the head with."

"I'd never use a book as a weapon!" *What a preposterous thought.*

"Well, that's good to know," said Blythe as he retrieved his stack from Rachel.

I craned my neck—stealthily, of course—to glimpse Blythe's library haul. Even though he was my sworn enemy, I still wanted to know what he was reading. I think I blushed when he caught me looking, for he made a grand show of concealing the covers with his arm as he slid them into his backpack.

"Okay, Thomas, naptime is over," said Rachel to her husband, the bookmobile driver. "We'll have to hurry if we want to arrive in Bright River on schedule. That means you kids need to clear out…unless Anne feels like being a stowaway on the bookmobile again."

"What? Anne…was a stowaway…on the bookmobile? Oh, this I gotta hear," said Blythe when he reached the bottom of the bus steps.

"Oh, it's *such* a good story," said Rachel. "It's heartwarming and heartbreaking all at the same time. Maybe Anne will tell it to you on your walk home." She then closed the bus doors.

I scurried away, not remotely interested in recounting the best and worst day of my life—and not to my sworn enemy, that's for certain.

Jogging a few steps, Blythe quickly caught up to me. I contemplated breaking into a run, but I knew it would be a lost cause. *Oh, why did I borrow so many heavy books this week?*

"Anne, what's this about stowing away on the bookmobile? I leave Avonlea for two years, under the safe assumption that nothing ever happens here. So you must understand how intrigued I am."

I continued to ignore him, and swatted at a mosquito instead.

"Nothing? But I've humbly apologized for my actions. Don't I get an apology in return? I'm the one who was physically injured, after all. That bump on my head is a real doozy. Or, at the very least, can't you forgive me?"

I halted in my tracks and turned to face my sworn enemy. "I shall never, ever forgive you or apologize to you, Gilbert Blythe!"

"Ah yes—the iron has entered into your soul. Diana warned me about that when I texted her. But I'm not too concerned. Now, if you'd said the *titanium* had entered into your soul—well, I'd have lost all hope of us being good friends someday. Avonlea is a small place, so I'll be seeing you, Anne."

"I'm so sorry I'm late!" I called out. "The geese got between me and my bike again. We'd still be in a standoff if Matthew hadn't distracted them." I wheeled my bike into the nearby boat shed and then bounded onto the dock.

"Oh, you're here," said Josie. "I was under the impression you couldn't come. My mom heard you were grounded—you know, for causing that food fight in the cafeteria. Gertie begged and begged to take your place. And what kind of sister would I be if I said no, especially to this adorable face?"

Gertie did her best impression of a pleading-face emoji.

"As you can see, I'm *not* grounded." I had a sneaking suspicion that Josie had created the miscommunication herself, but I wasn't going to let her ruin my fun. "I'm so excited! I've never been paddleboarding before."

"Oh, we've already claimed and paid for our paddleboards, and there isn't an extra one available," said Josie. "But there might be a way for you to tag along," she added, brushing past me. She hopped from the dock to the pond's edge and then knelt to examine a moored rowboat. She called out, "Anne can take this one, can't she, Charlie?"

That's when I remembered Charlie Sloane was working as an attendant for the paddleboard business. Other than the fact Charlie was in our grade at school, I knew nothing else about him. I turned to him expectantly. However, I refused to reshape my features into a plead-ing-face emoji. I had *some* dignity.

"I…I guess so," said Charlie. "You'll have to return it to the dock when you're done, though. It's too awkward to move it over land. Blythe is waiting downstream to transport the paddleboards and your friends by tractor when they're finished."

What? Blythe works at the paddleboard business, too? Why does Avonlea have to be so small?

"Oh, I don't mind rowing back at all," I said. *Anything to avoid bumping into Blythe.*

"We can't wait any longer. We're heading out!" shouted Josie.

"Bye, Anne!" called Ruby and Jane, waving halfheart-edly to me.

Never mind, I have my imagination to keep me company…again.

"Anne, would you like me to take your backpack for you and keep it safe in the boat shed?" asked Charlie.

I jumped. I'd almost forgotten Charlie Sloane was even there. I was just about to relinquish my backpack when I noticed the name painted on the side of the rowboat: *The Lily Maid.*

Now, why does that sound familiar? Oh, I've got it! It's from the Tennyson poem. How interesting...

"No, I'll take my stuff with me. That's very thoughtful of you to ask, though, Charlie."

As I rummaged around in my backpack for some money to pay for the rowboat rental, I suddenly felt the need to make small talk. I hated awkward silences almost as much as I hated my hair colour. "So, Charlie, how was the rental business this summer?"

"Oh, it was terrible, just terrible, Anne. We can't seem to attract any tourists to Avonlea, or to Prince Edward Island for that matter. It's like we don't even exist to the rest of the world. Here's your lifejacket, Anne."

"Oh, thanks, Charlie, but I don't need your help putting it on. I can manage." I then carefully stepped into the rowboat and pushed away from shore. "Bye, Charlie!"

"Bon voyage, Anne! If you're not back in half an hour, I'll send a search party for you."

"Let's hope it doesn't come to that!" I called out.

Charlie Sloane talked like an old man trapped in a twelve-year-old's body. *Don't be so hard on him*, I scolded myself. *He may not be kindred-spirit material, but he's friendly at least.*

To my dismay, I was not a natural-born rower. I kept going in circles. Quitting was not an option, however,

what with Charlie shouting words of encouragement and advice into his megaphone from the dock. I didn't want to disappoint my cheerleading squad of one. I got the hang of it…eventually. When Charlie and the dock became a speck in the distance, I let myself drink in my surroundings.

Ah, the shining waters, the electric blue sky, the dragonflies darting to and fro, the cattails waving in the gentle breeze… Oh, there's an island up ahead. I wonder…No, I shouldn't. Then again…how many rowboats in the world are named The Lily Maid? *Yes, I must.*

I grabbed my cell and selfie stick from my bag and then lay back in the rowboat. *Except…lifejackets weren't invented in the days of Camelot. And it's important to be as authentic as possible when doing a reenactment, so maybe I'll slip out of it for just a moment. Wait, I'm missing something. I can't very well be Elaine, the lily maid, without…*I slid my hand into my backpack and pulled out some wildflowers I had picked earlier. *A ditch lily? Its orange petals seem too cheerful. A white lily would be better. Not to mention, my red hair is all wrong. And…action!*

Is it just my imagination or am I now soaking wet? I must not have noticed the water at the bottom of the boat when I boarded. Satisfied that I had captured the scene on my cell, I sat up and opened my eyes. *What! The boat is sinking! And my lifejacket is floating away!*

I stopped recording and then stuffed my cell and selfie stick in my backpack. I had three options: sink, swim, or strand myself on the nearby tiny island with the cattails

and wait for rescue. *Swim it is!* Holding my backpack above water, I did my mightiest eggbeater kick. *Terra firma, here I come!*

Cold, exhausted, and drenched, I crawled up the bank, hauling my backpack behind me. I was the very definition of bedraggled.

"Fancy bumping into you so soon. I told you Avonlea is small."

"Gilbert Blythe! What are you doing here, lurking about?"

"Lurking about? I don't think so. When you didn't return on time, Charlie sent out a search party. That's me. I'm the search party."

"Well, you found me. Congratulations." I gave him my best stink eye.

"You're not going to apologize for sinking my rowboat?" Blythe plopped down on the mossy bank beside me.

"Apologize? For sinking an obviously defective boat?"

"Didn't you see the 'out of order' sign?" asked Blythe. "The rowboat was off-limits."

It finally hit me. Of course. Josie Pye. I squared my shoulders and turned to him. "Gilbert Blythe, I humbly apologize for sinking your rowboat. It wasn't my intention, of course. I saw *The Lily Maid* painted on the side, and I couldn't resist taking it out. It's from my favourite poem, 'Lancelot and Elaine'—or one of them. I have a lot of favourites."

"Really? It was my mother's favourite, too."

"*Was?*" All I could hear was the past tense of his verb. "It *was* your mother's favourite?" My voice was barely above a whisper.

"Yeah, she died about two years ago."

"Oh, I'm so sorry, Blythe. I know what it's like to lose someone. My parents died when I was a baby. I never even had a chance to get to know them."

"I knew we'd have something in common, though this is one thing I wish we didn't." He cleared his throat. "Uh, if it's okay with you, I'm changing the topic. So…nice eggbeater kick. Impressive display of upper arm strength, too, getting your backpack to land without submerging it."

"Why, thank you," I said, fluttering my hands in mock appreciation. "I guess those aquafit classes with three sets of Hammond twins really paid off," I added with a laugh.

Wait. I'm laughing…and not AT Gilbert Blythe, but WITH him. Hmm…maybe I should remove him from my list of sworn enemies. I sank his rowboat, after all.

Seeing his confusion, I continued, "In my second-last foster family, I helped take care of three sets of twins. I still have nightmares where I'm chasing after them." Clutching a nearby tree branch, I lurched to my feet. Blythe stood up, too.

"Here, let me carry your backpack for you," he offered. Before I could stop him, he grabbed it, causing my cell and selfie stick to slip out onto the ground.

"Anne, were you *filming* something? Something for our art project, by chance?" he said, bending to retrieve my

cell.

"Give me that!" I said, a little too forcibly.

"Need I remind you that you sank my rowboat, named after my dear—"

I threw my hands up in defeat. "Okay, okay, you're right—it's for our art project. I was reenacting Elaine's death journey to Camelot. Fine. You can watch it. But keep in mind, it hasn't been edited."

Blythe moved into the shadows cast by the trees to watch the clip. Suddenly his shoulders shook. He placed one hand on the tree for support and gasped for air.

Is he overcome with emotion? Is my performance that moving? Wait…is he…LAUGHING?

The iron entered once more into my soul.

I snatched my cell from him, slung my backpack over my shoulders, and stormed off, my sneakers making embarrassing squishing sounds with each stomp of my feet on the path.

Blythe quickly caught up. My soaked clothing was hindering my storming off. "Anne, please stop and watch the clip. If not for my sake, then for my dear—"

"All right, all right." With an exaggerated sigh, I opened my phone and watched what I had intended to be a haunting performance.

I bit my lip and then clamped my hand over my mouth, but it was no use. "Okay…it's…funny…I … admit…it," I said between giggles.

"I know—the look on your face when you finally, *finally* realized the boat was sinking! I mean, that's pure

comedy gold. So, you *do* have a sense of humour. Diana claimed you did, but I was beginning to doubt her. Okay, I have an idea. How about we film reenactments of famous book scenes for our art project? Or…do you still want to work separately?"

At that moment, we emerged from the woods onto a dirt road. From a tractor parked nearby, Blythe lifted my bike from the attached wagon.

"No, working together makes sense—even I can admit that. At the very least, you can hold the camera steady." I reached for my bike as Blythe set it on the ground.

"Yeah, your shaky camera made me want to puke," he said. "Okay, make a list of your favourite books, and email it to me. I'll let you know if I've read any of them. Trust me, you won't regret this, Anne. Now, I'd better go before Charlie sends out a search party for me."

All clear—Marilla was at the bakery, Matthew was in the orchard, and, most importantly, the geese were nowhere in sight. I stood on the sandstone step and pinched myself.

Yes, Green Gables does exist. And I'm the luckiest girl in the world…despite my ridiculous red hair.

Glancing over my shoulder, I noticed I'd left a trail of wet footprints on the sandstone step. *Hmm…maybe they'll dry before Matthew and Marilla come home. I'd rather they didn't know about my latest misadventure. Oh, who am I kidding? I'm sure half of Avonlea already knows.*

I hurried upstairs, quickly changed into dry clothes, and then turned on my laptop. I just happened to have a list of my favourite books on file. *Hmm…what do I say to Blythe?* Normally, I was never at a loss for words, so this was a new experience for me. I told myself it was just an email: Keep it brief. Keep it professional. So I simply typed "Your thoughts?" in the subject line. *Hmm… succinct, direct, concise—my English teacher would be proud of me.* As I clicked on my list to include as an attachment, I was startled by a commotion outside. *Will no one rid me of these turbulent geese?* I fumed.

To my surprise, Blythe responded within minutes. His reply was not quite as succinct as mine, but close:

So. Many. Thoughts. Meet me outside Marilla's bakery @ 4:45.

"Plum puff?" said Blythe. He was standing in the shade of a maple tree, near the bakery.

"No, thanks. Wait, yes. I can't resist Marilla's plum puffs." I then reached into the proffered brown paper bag and drew out one. "Um…what are your…many thoughts?" I asked between bites.

"Well, Anne—or should I say, 'Rosamond Montmo-rency'?"

I nearly choked on my plum puff. "How…how do you know my nom de plume? Did Diana mention it? Oh no, why would she do that?"

"Diana didn't tell me anything. You did…when you attached that short story to your email. I had no idea you're a writer…and that you know so much about the daily lives of lords and ladies." Blythe popped an entire plum puff into his mouth and chewed.

I slumped against the tree and slid down its trunk to the ground. I then buried my face in my hands. "I'm so mortified. I must have clicked on the wrong document when I was distracted by the geese squawking outside. Why do I keep getting into these scrapes?"

"Mortified? Scrapes?" echoed Blythe, sitting down beside me. "No one our age uses those words. Why do you sound like you've stepped out of the Victorian era? You're not a time traveller, are you? I won't tell anyone if you are."

I glanced up. There he was, waggling his eyebrows at me again. "Ha ha. No, I'm not a time traveller, though I'd love to be. I just read a lot of old books."

"Ah yes. Rachel Lynde mentioned something about you being in the middle of a classic literature phase. Another plum puff?" He held out the bag.

I considered his offer, but declined.

"I'm too mortified to eat. Um…what did you think of my story? You can give me your honest opinion. I've read it's important for writers to receive constructive feedback. So…fire away." I leaned back against the tree, awaiting his inevitable praise.

"Well, okay, I…I couldn't relate to any of the charac-

ters—you know, because they're lords and ladies. They were so pompous and self-absorbed. And the hero, ugh, what did the main character see in him, anyway? He was so serious—no sense of humour, whatsoever. I felt sorry for the villain, though. I mean, I wouldn't wish death by a thousand paper cuts on anyone, especially since antibiotics hadn't been invented yet." Blythe didn't hold back.

"So, you think my story was terrible! I'll never write anything ever again!" I was on my feet in an instant and went to grab my bike and leave.

"Ow!" I yelped as something hit my back. "What was *that* for?"

"I had to get your attention somehow. It's too bad a poor plum puff had to be sacrificed in the process, though. Look, I never said you should stop writing—far from it. I thought your 'Chaos in the Cafeteria' account was brilliant. And referring to me as 'Wretched Boy' was…hilarious. That's the kind of stuff you should write about, you know, your everyday mistakes—or your scrapes, as you like to call them." Blythe seemed pretty sincere, so I paused for a moment to consider what he said.

"Really?" Relief flooded over me. "You think people would find that interesting?"

"Yeah, I do. Who knows, if you experience some more scrapes, you might have enough material for a novel. You might even put Prince Edward Island on the map someday. For instance…I'm intrigued as to how you became a stowaway on the bookmobile." Blythe must

have noticed my reluctance to share anything personal, for he added, "I could reveal something about myself in exchange. Like, I'm willing to divulge what books I borrowed from the bookmobile today. I know you're dying to find out."

As if Blythe's book haul is as personally revealing as my stowaway tale.

My bibliocuriosity, however, got the better of me.

"Okay, okay, you win." I took a deep breath before beginning my Avonlea origin story. "I'd just moved in with a new foster family in White Sands, and I was asked by my foster mom to go to the store to buy some groceries. I had every intention of doing so, but I got distracted by the bookmobile in the parking lot. That's when I witnessed Rachel Lynde informing Marilla and Matthew about the ins and outs of operating the bookmobile. You see, her husband, Thomas, suddenly wasn't feeling well, so she called in Matthew and Marilla to carry out their duties and finish the day's run. In all the commotion, I slipped into the bookmobile and stowed away, unbeknownst to Matthew and Marilla until they discovered me at the next stop."

"And you charmed them so much that they adopted you on the spot," interrupted Blythe. "Hmm…that explains the heartwarming part of the story, but Rachel mentioned something about it being heartbreaking, too."

"Well, they didn't adopt me on the spot. It doesn't work that way. I had to go back to the Blewett family that evening, without the groceries." I paused, wondering how

much I wanted to reveal. "Uh, which…annoyed them greatly."

"Did you say the Blewett family of White Sands?" said Blythe, gripping my arm. "Because they've been up on numerous charges. When I was travelling with my dad, I remember reading news from the Island that a foster kid even ran away from them. Wait…that was you."

I stared upward at the gorgeous blue sky. *Go to your happy place. Go to your happy place. Go to your happy place.*

Blythe released his grip on my arm. "Anne, where did you just go?"

I shook my head and flashed him a half-smile. "Oh, nowhere. I was thinking about Green Gables, that's all. I'm sorry—what were we talking about?"

"The fact that you ran away—"

I fluttered my hands in mild protest. "It wasn't so much as running away as…searching for kindred spirits."

"Kindred spirits? There you go again, talking like a Victorian time traveller."

"A kindred spirit is someone with similar interests to yours. No, it's more than that. It's someone you have a deep connection with. That's why I read so many books. I'm looking for kindred spirits in the pages. Some of my best friends are book characters. Oh, that just made me sound pathetic. Forget I said that."

"No, I get it—you're searching for your people. I just hope you find them in your real life, too."

"Oh, I have! Matthew and Marilla and Diana, they're all kindred spirits. Okay, now it's your turn. Show me

your book haul. And tell me why you read so many books."

"Well, I'm not searching for kindred spirits, but I am on a quest. You see, before my mom died, she gave me a list of books to read. It…helps me feel connected to her," said Blythe, opening his backpack to reveal its contents.

"That's my favourite!" I couldn't believe what I was looking at. "I'm surprised—no, gobsmacked—you're reading *Pride and Prejudice*." But then my face fell when the book's full title came into view. "Ew…*and Zombies*." I grimaced as though I had mistakenly bitten into a turnip.

"Anne, are you…a book snob? The irony! Your favourite book is *Pride and Prejudice*, and you're *prejudiced* against certain types of books. Don't go shaking your head in denial. Admitting it is the first step. That's it—book snobbery will be the topic of our next video." Blythe zipped up his backpack to hide the offending object.

At that moment, Marilla flipped the "open" sign to "closed" and exited the bakery.

"I gotta go," said Blythe, shouldering his backpack before I had a chance to pass judgment on his other books. "Bye, Anne. Anne with an 'e.'"

Marilla materialized next to me. "You certainly had lots to talk about with Gilbert Blythe, considering he's your sworn enemy."

I picked my bike off the ground and then fell into step beside her for our walk home.

"Oh, he's no longer my sworn enemy. That would be a bad idea when we're working on an art project together," I

said with a laugh. "You know what, Marilla? I discovered something today."

"And what would that be, Anne?"

"Kindred spirits aren't as scarce as I once thought. They're out there. You just need to keep searching until you find them."

When **Hope Dalvay** read *Anne of Green Gables* at the age of ten, she knew she had found her BFF (her Best Fictional Friend) in Anne Shirley. Later, Hope turned her daydreaming habit into a passion for writing middle-grade children's novels (*Welcome to Camp Fill-in-the-Blank* and *My Year as a SPACE Cadet*) and an educational picture book (*The Multiplication Rap*). Her short story "In Search of Kindred Spirits" (*The ANNEthology*) is an expression of Hope's heartfelt gratitude to the friend and to the book that made her a forever reader. Visit Hope on Instagram and Twitter @hopedalvay, or on Facebook at Hope Dalvay or Hope Dalvay Author.

PAUL COCCIA

Carpetbaggers

Do they have it in the bag?

To Lena

The old argument between optimists and pessimists comes into my mind as I pick up my thrift store carpetbag. It, too, is half-full (or half-empty depending on your alignment), its thick fabric and heavy leather handles weighing more than its contents: an extra pair of jeans, a few shirts, a comb, deodorant, toothbrush and paste, and a plastic water bottle so full it leaves no room for debates. Hidden inside my jeans for protection is a dollar store frame housing the only photograph of my mother and me, her newborn barely taking up any space in her arms.

Thinking about how I want to fill the rest of my life, I adjust my grip. The bag's leather handles are worn down in places from a previous owner or owners and yet fit my hand as if I had been the one to break them in. I'm sure the bag looks as if it belongs to someone's grandmother, not something that would appeal to a sixteen-year-old boy, with its muted floral pattern and coarse material thinning in spots from age and wear. Still, the proportions of my bag and its bulk fit me and my frame. I hold out my ticket to the attendant as I step up onto the train, my new used bag held firmly before me.

Once I'm through the entrance area of the train where passengers stow larger pieces of luggage, I choose an optimal seat, close enough to the bathrooms to know if they're empty, but far enough not to hear what anyone may do in them.

My hips spread out into all the available space, and my love handles bulge onto the armrests as I wedge myself into the window seat. I look around at the near-empty car and pray it stays that way for the rest of the journey. I don't want to fold and compress myself as small as I possibly can, leaning away from the passenger beside me to give them more room. I'd like to travel without crushing myself up, without feeling I'm not entitled to the space I fill by wholes, not halves.

As the train pushes forward, there is no fanfare, no sudden lurch ahead to skip along the rails and propel me toward my destiny. No, the train moves with deliberate intention, a measured, considered pace that gradually picks up speed and gains momentum. Maybe that's how life is, too. Even so, I wish the train would somehow lift from its tracks, transporting my grandest dreams into blue skies and clouds mounded like freshly whipped Chantilly cream. Taking me to the guy at the other end. My guy, maybe, if he'll have me. But the train stays safely rooted to the earth and makes my body rock and bump and jiggle.

I look out my window. The scenery blurs past. Hopeton is now behind me. No sense pressing my sweaty forehead against the pane of glass and leaving a greasy smear as there's no way I could see the town from the

train anyway. Aware I'm perspiring, I wipe the back of my hand against my forehead before rubbing it on the thigh of my jeans. I don't need anyone noticing me all shiny and gross. I should feel a sense of sadness or loss or relief or anything at all. But I don't. I know it was only a temporary place. Ephemeral. Transient. Limbo. Somewhere to be until I was old enough to make my way anywhere else.

It turns out that despite all the books and movies and TV shows of orphans who can charm even the most reluctant of guardians, my red hair and positive attitude weren't enough to secure me a real home in Hopeton after Bertha died. Instead, I was passed off to anyone who would take me. In the end, the promise of a government cheque and a pair of hands to help with her brood is what motivated Mrs. Hammond's philanthropy. I was an easier sell as a foster if I had some added perks attached, especially ones preceded by dollar signs.

But now I'm on my own and on an adventure. I hope a life—my life—can finally start this very second, even if it is only a half-full one.

A sour-faced woman appears in the aisle, pushing a wobbly metal trolley that's built like a tank with the dents and scrapes to prove it. As the two pass, I can see cellophaned sandwiches with white labels listing ingredients, chocolate bars with wrinkled wrappers, and a few cans of soda sweating with condensation. I spread my knees from where they're pressed against the back of the seat in front of me to fish a laminated menu out of the pocket where it

is filed along with a sick sac. I scan the prices. Everything is out of my budget, not that anything is enticing. I spent almost all my money on the ticket. One way. No take-backs.

The train stops at the first station along the route. A few new passengers board. None, thankfully, sit beside me. I consider putting my bag up onto the empty seat, a nonverbal message that a companion is not wanted or welcome.

Just thinking that, I can almost hear Mrs. Hammond all the way from Hopeton scolding me. "*Don't even think about it. You're not entitled to two seats, Anne. You're already spilling out of the one you paid for.*" She'd turn to Mr. Hammond. "*Go on, Kendrick. Tell him.*"

I leave my bag stowed under the chair in front of me. No one wants to sit beside me, anyway.

The train takes off again and I crane my neck to look toward the front of the car. The other passengers play on their phones or read books and magazines. One pair is asleep, heads resting against one another. They're either a couple or the closest of bosom friends as their heads gently jostle against one another—one on top, one nestled underneath—with every bump of the track.

I cross my arms on top of my belly. Like the rest of me, my arms are so freckled that my pale skin peeks out in slivers and slices. If someone decided to map my skin and compare percentages, I think freckles would end up beating out the plain areas.

Outside the window, the farmland is dotted with trees

and grass, ponds whizzing by. I'm not at all tired, but I try to close my eyes and convince myself to sleep. Even a catnap would be good, as I was up most of the night before thinking about what meeting him would be like.

At first, he will be shocked. How could he not be? He'll wrap me in his arms, kiss my cheek, then hold me at arm's length for a good, long look.

My gut jiggles with a bump on the tracks. I'm a lot to take in. But he'll beam at me and pull me with him to sit, my hand clasped in his, smiling as we get to know one another properly, in some disbelief I'm finally in front of him, that we're finally together at last. He'll ask me questions like…How did I manage to find him? What took me so long? Where have I been? I'll tell him my tale. He'll gasp and be impressed at all the right parts. We will laugh and our sides will press against one another, as comfortable and as meant-to-be as the sleeping duo a few rows in front of me.

I try to rest, but sleep evades me. So instead, I stand and stretch, holding the front hem of my T-shirt down so my belly doesn't show. My calves feel tight and burn from having been compressed and, now, forcibly stretched out. I decide to head to the washroom and end up shimmying sideways through the narrow aisle to avoid knocking my gut or butt into people as I lurch from the motion of the train toward the rear of the car. I don't think anyone would make a nasty comment about my weight, but I can also imagine they'd glare at me the rest of the trip with silent judgment.

The washroom is tiny. There's barely enough room to stand in front of the toilet and the ledge of the sink presses against my left thigh. When I lift the lid, part of me expects to stare into the bowl and see the tracks whizzing by below. But it's a regular toilet, no peekaboo view.

I undo my jeans and pull the front of my underwear down when the train forcefully rocks to the side. As I sway left and right, I clench every muscle in my groin. I can imagine myself spraying everywhere like a garden hose a child turns on too high and drops, not able to control. I'm afraid I'll be knocked off my feet, ending up drenched and trapped in the standing space between the door and toilet base. Once I was found, someone would have to unhinge the door to pry me out like a sardine.

While standing to go is always the option I use in a public washroom, I've got no other choice here. Quickly, I make myself a nest of toilet paper, suck in my breath and my gut, and manage to turn, yanking down my pants and underwear in one motion before I plunk down on top of the bucking throne. It doesn't matter that the metal handrails crush my thighs, I grab onto them as the train bucks back and forth again, praying I won't be unseated. I remain sitting to wash my hands when I am done.

An older lady smiles at me from across the aisle as I ease my way back into my seat.

"Those bathrooms should come with an instruction manual," she says. "Or a warning label."

I give a half-smile in agreement as I pull my bag from

under the seat and reach in, rummaging around until I find the bottle of water. I refilled it on the platform before boarding. It's still cool. I'm careful to only take one sip. I don't want a repeat of the bathroom performance.

After we pass several more stations, the trolley woman finally reappears. She pushes a stray hair off her forehead with the back of her hand as she leans into the handle and shoves the cart down the aisle, stopping to take orders, accept payments, and make change.

When the trolley woman gets to my row, she says, "No more sandwiches. They never send enough. I'm always out before the last two cars. I've got pretzels, pop, and a couple of Mars bars if you're interested."

The lady across the aisle says, "No, thank you," and returns to her reading.

I look at the cart and imagine Mrs. Hammond again. *"Candy and sweets? You certainly don't need any more of those."*

I shake my head as I slide my plastic water bottle between my thigh and the armrest with a loud crunch.

The trolley woman's eyes travel down to the worn bag peeking out next to my old sneakers.

"First time on a train?" she asks.

I nod.

"Going to the city?"

I nod again.

"First time for that, too?"

I stare up at her. I remember having it drilled into me as a kid not to talk to strangers. Mrs. Hammond would

have muttered, *"What does she want to know for? Doesn't she have enough of her own business to mind without getting into yours?"*

This woman, however, seems intent on a conversation. I answer, "Yes. I'm going to meet someone."

"Exciting," she deadpans. "Family?"

I hesitate. She's asking a lot of personal questions. Thinking of Mrs. Hammond, I pick a true but vague answer. "I guess. Sort of. Not exactly."

She nods this time as if she knows what I mean. She fishes around her cart, before tossing me a box of Smarties. "I ran over them. They're still perfectly good inside even if the box is messed up. On the house, kid."

"Thanks." I tear open the corner of the box and pour a couple of them into my palm, then pop them into my mouth. The candy-coated shells crack between my molars and chocolate floods across my tongue.

She smiles. "Remember—eat the red ones last."

With a small grunt, she leans forward and pushes her cart farther down the aisle to inform the rest of the passengers that she's out of sandwiches.

When we finally arrive in the city, I slide my carpetbag onto my forearm and take my place in the queue to exit. The lady near me stands, using the seats in front of her for support as she unfolds. I position myself to create a roadblock and give her a chance to step out into the aisle before the passengers behind us surge forward.

Stepping onto the indoor platform, I gaze up. The ceilings skyrocket above me. The tracks stretch out with

several trains huffing away, waiting to be released toward their next destinations. People are hurrying, children are crying, luggage is banging or clacking along. Someone must be smoking nearby because the fiery odor wafts in. It's faint and not unpleasant, familiar like camping and roasting marshmallows.

I only have a moment to look around before getting bumped forward. I end up joining the crowd, which carries and pushes me with it from the platform into the station. People flow around me. There are no dirty looks or rude comments about moving out of the way or what an inconvenience I am to get around. People barely seem to notice me. It's as if I'm one of the pillars or benches. I feel my lips turn up and begin to hum quietly to myself.

I follow the crowd through the double doors. Many are hurrying into another station, going from train to subway. Maybe I should do the same, but I'm not exactly sure where I am or how to get to where I need to be. My carpetbag knocks against my hip and thigh, reminding me it's there. The bag is my only companion to see me through this trip and whatever happens.

I wander along the path between the stations until I find a pile of two-by-fours stacked outside a chain-link fence. I perch on top of them as gingerly as a big guy can, my bag beside me, its handles nestled in the crook of my elbow. I pry my phone out of my pocket where it's wedged, trying to shield the screen with my hand from the glare so I can pull up a map. I sigh, not able to see anything.

"You can't sit there, buddy," a man in a hard hat and neon orange and yellow safety vest says.

I scramble to my feet, ready to apologize.

"Calm down, son. You know where you're going?"

"It's that obvious?" I ask.

He pulls a pack of cigarettes from his back pocket and knocks one out. He cups his hand around the tip as the cigarette hangs from his lips, then clicks a lighter. The end of the cigarette glows red before he puffs out and smoke trails up.

"You want one?" he asks.

"No. I'm not old enough."

"Good boy. Neither was I when I picked it up. Don't start. It's a bad habit. Too expensive."

"Why don't you quit?"

He takes another drag. "Where are you trying to get to? I'll point you in the right direction."

I hesitate but figure if this rugged construction worker is going to respond negatively, I can't control that and will deal with the outcome. "The Village," I blurt out.

"The *Gay* Village," I add, waiting for his reaction.

He nods as he takes another puff. He points. "Walk five blocks that way. Then go left and keep walking until you're there."

"But how will I know I'm there?"

He laughs. "You'll know. No mistaking it." He takes a final drag and flicks his cigarette butt into the gutter beside the curb. "And, son? Be careful. I wasn't old enough to smoke once, too, if you get my meaning." He

lowers his wraparound sunglasses enough to give me a wink. "I might catch you there later tonight. Have fun. Go get yourself into some trouble."

I can't help but grin. I want to race on, but I know I won't last more than half a block if I run. He's here. I'm here. In the same city. Blocks apart. Kindred spirits—I'm sure we must be—about to meet at last.

Soon I'm plodding, wondering how much longer there is to go and if I took a wrong turn somewhere. My inner thighs begin to burn from the friction of rubbing together and my shirt feels damp. A trickle of sweat goes down the small of my back and down my cleft below that. Although there's not much in it, I've switched my bag from hand to hand to give my fingers a chance to relax. Perhaps I should ask someone else if they know where the Village is, but would they be as cool as the construction guy?

However, just like the construction guy told me, I know I'm in the right place when the rainbows start appearing. At first, it's only a small rainbow sticker on the door of a restaurant. Some twinkling lights. A flag waving from up high on a balcony. Then another. And another. Banners on every lamppost. Every crosswalk in every intersection painted with more rainbows. Every awning is draped with sparkling fringe. Even people seem to appear as if on cue, coming out of condos, restaurants, and shops, creating their own spectrum when viewed as a whole, as if they are light being refracted through a prism.

I look away as I pass a shop with items in the window I could never imagine seeing anywhere back in Hopeton.

But the part of me that wants to know what's there causes me to stop in front on the middle of the sidewalk. I lift my head, turn to face the window, and unabashedly gaze in. A mannequin strapped in leather and other various items, instruments, and wares poses proudly on display. My blaze of red hair reflects back at me. Red for life. I see my body in the glass, too. It envelops the mannequin, superimposed, our proportions drastically different. My carpetbag, mirrored in the window, dangles from the mannequin's fingers. I quickly turn away.

"Excuse me," I say to the nearest guy sipping coffee at a metal café table. "Do you know where The Gables is?"

He raises an eyebrow and then jerks his head across the street. "Green awning over there. But they're strict. They won't let a chicken like you in. You'd be eaten alive."

I thank him and look both ways before crossing the street against the red light and up the stairs of The Gables.

No one is seated at the stool by the door under a sign that warns "Government ID with a photo and birthdate must be shown upon request. You must be at least 19 or older to enter."

Undeterred, I peek around the corner into the dimly lit bar. The dark wood is lacquered to a high gloss. The walls, floors, and bar tops gleam. Most of the light comes from the sliding glass doors of the narrow balconies.

He's in here somewhere. I know it. He has to be. And we'll finally meet. Face-to-face at last. A brand-new chapter in my life. In both our lives. Our fate unraveling before us in this very spot.

Except he doesn't know I'm here. I didn't give him a warning. I couldn't bear the thought of him sending me a message telling me not to come. An excuse on why we shouldn't meet. It was a risk I wasn't willing to take in this whole plan. I have to know, not by text or DM, but in real time, in real person, where we stand and what we can be to each other.

I'd researched his social media feed, which sounds a lot better than I cyber-stalked him, and found pictures of him with a bunch of other gay guys in this very bar, The Gables. They were drinking and joking and laughing, arms around one another, posing for the cameras, duck-face selfies, big smiles, good times. Their toned arms in tight tees and tanks. His shirt with The Gables' logo across one flexed pec as he poured drinks behind the bar.

I swallow hard and step deeper into the bar. My sneakers don't make any sound. I scan the place for someone, anyone.

A guy in a cropped jersey stretched over his broad, muscular chest and shoulders comes out from a back room, carrying two cases of beer. I can barely see his face under his beard and ball cap.

Stepping forward, I raise my hand to wave, but he spots me before I have a chance.

"We don't open for another half hour." He stares at me. "And you're not old enough. You shouldn't be here." He lifts the cases and uses his shoulder to push the first onto the top of the bar.

"Let me help you," I say, hoping to win him over with

the small gesture. I go to put down my bag so I can take the second case, but he's got it up before I can even touch it.

The guy glares at me, then nods at the door.

"Is Matthew working tonight? Matthew Cuthbert?" I ask before the guy has a chance to tell me, unequivocally, to leave.

The guy pushes the brim of his cap up as he slowly looks me over. The silence fills in the space between us.

"Matthew, eh?" he finally says. "Give me a second."

I step farther into the bar as the muscled guy returns to the back room. I tilt my head up to see myself staring up in the slanted mirrors across the entire bar ceiling. My red hair. My skin, mostly freckles. The roll of my belly and the dent of my navel under my shirt. My soft man boobs, nipples hard from the air-conditioning. Pit stains bleeding out from under my arms. I tug at my T-shirt, then rub my nipples hoping to make them go down. They only get worse. The floral bag, looking deflated and lumpy at the same time, repeats overhead infinitely.

I gaze up once more and, as I lower my head, catch myself looking down on me.

From his photos, I know Matthew is handsome. He's cool. He's always got friends around him. He must be popular. He's always smiling. He's out and he's proud.

Maybe I could have all of that, too. Maybe I could be like him. I want more than to be a charity case. A foster kitten. Mired in Hopeton. A fat, freckled kid afraid to come out because even if I did, what's back there for me?

What future? There is only limited potential where I've come from. I want more. I can be more.

But what if Matthew doesn't like what he sees? What if I'm too much? Any photos he received aren't recent. What if he takes one look and tells me to go? I can't be what he imagined. What he hoped for. What he would choose if given some other option, any other option.

But while I might be a nervous, undesirable kid, I'm not too afraid to stand in front of Matthew and take the chance that maybe, just maybe, he sees something he likes. That instead of the sweat and the boobs and the belly and a worn old bag and the uncertainty, he'll see someone worth getting to know. Someone who maybe is worth wanting. Someone that could belong to him. We all need to belong to someone. Why can't I belong to him?

The muscled guy returns with a tall, skinny man with an earpiece who reminds me of Jack Skellington.

"I see what you meant," the skinny guy whispers, but I can hear him clear as anything across the empty bar.

"You're looking for Matthew?" the skinny guy asks. "He's upstairs. Hurry up, now. We open soon and I really shouldn't allow you in. We could end up in a lot of trouble."

I tuck my bag against my side and rush after the skinny guy, who doesn't wait for me or look back to see if I'm following. We pass through a door behind a second bar and then up a staircase that bends at a landing, then bends again and again as we climb up into The Gables.

The skinny guy knocks at the door. "Marilla?" he calls. He knocks once more when there's no answer. "You decent, sis?"

"I came for Matthew. Matthew Cuthbert," I say.

"You want Matthew, you get Marilla. Package deal." The skinny guy opens the door and pokes his head in. "Someone you'll want to see is here."

"I'm not properly done up yet. I'll take fans later. Tell them to come back." Matthew's voice is muffled through the door.

The skinny guy pats my shoulder. "Go on in. It will be OK."

My hand hesitates on the doorknob before I push the door open and step inside. There's a lit tri-fold mirror on a cheap folding table. Someone sits on a metal chair in front of it, leaning forward, a brush flying rapidly across their face. The door swings fully open behind me.

The person looks over their shoulder. "I said I wasn't ready—holy shit!"

His eyes narrow then widen. He turns, a shiny dressing robe falls off his shoulders to drag along the ground. His shaved chest fully visible above the corset. The lines of the makeup on his face unblended. His red hair slicked back against his skull.

He looks almost unrecognizable. "Matthew?" I ask.

"Shit!" Matthew repeats as he smacks his brush onto the table. "Of all the stupid times to be sober." He crosses the room to lean past me, open the door and shout down the stairs, "Tell Minnie May to get her ass ready to get on that stage. She's first now. I need a minute." He squares off in front of me. "What are you doing here?"

I gulp and place my bag between our bodies. His skin that isn't covered by makeup is freckled.

"I came to meet you," I manage to say.

"No. No way. Bertha and I had an agreement."

"An agreement?"

"She wanted a baby. I had the goods. It's not as if I wasn't already giving it away to a bunch of guys back then. Or now for that matter. So why shouldn't she benefit from a little of it?" He picks up a brush and goes to sit down, stops himself, then turns to face me again. "That's not the point though. She promised—no, she swore—I wasn't to be involved. You can't be showing up, willy-nilly, out of the blue. How the hell did you even find me?"

I lower my hand, letting my bag hang at my side. I use my thumb to rub the leather handles. "My mom's journals. She mentioned your name enough times around when she would have gotten pregnant. So, I Googled you." But I'd only found Matthew Cuthbert. No mention of Marilla. I'd have remembered Marilla. "I thought you were a bartender."

"When I'm not a headliner," Matthew says with a flourish of his arms. He walks back to the folding table and bends down, picking up a wig and flipping it back as he straightens up. The lace mesh sticks out from his forehead. "Marilla. Matthew. One and the same." He swings his hips as he comes toward me, sweeping his arms

down in front of his body. As he stops, he bends his knee, his leg slipping forward through the slit of his robe.

I suck my bottom lip and roll it back and forth between my teeth.

Matthew crosses his arms over his chest and leans back slightly, one of his hips jutting to the side. "You look like her. The way you chew on your lip like that. And the ears. And the eyes." He drops his arms. "God, she was fun. Wild. Untamed. We did so many things we shouldn't have." He gestures toward me. "Point in case." He shakes his head, then leans forward so he can glue the wig's lace down. "I don't know what you want from me."

I am silent for a moment, trying to figure out how to sell the idea, how to sell myself to this man. "I won't be any trouble. I only need a place to stay. Just for a little while."

"Listen, kid, Miss Marilla is a lone wolf and Matthew's even less fussy on commitment. I did my part and was done. Bertha got her baby. No strings. No obligations. No Matthew. No sirree. Where is she anyway? Did she put you up to this? That would be so like her."

I hesitate. "She died." I pause. "Years ago. I couldn't get here any sooner."

The silence draws and stretches out like the train tracks. I can't think of anything to say to salvage this moment that's quickly derailing.

"Shit. Just. Shit," Matthew mumbles.

"It's OK. I'm here now. And you're my father."

He laughs. "I don't think so. I'm no one's father. I'm

not fit for it. I can barely take care of myself." He reaches up as if to hold his head in his hand but purses his lips as he remembers his makeup. "Grab a chair and sit down. I've got to finish getting my face and costume on. Listen, kid, I'm going to be real with you. I don't want you expecting nothing of me. Got it? I'm not what you want. I sure as hell can't be. I'll send you back to wherever you came from. We'll keep going on with our lives, the same as before. Like this never happened."

I shake my head. It has happened. "I can't go back there," I say. "Not to the Hammonds and Hopeton. Not now that we've met. You and me, we're the same." And behind that last word is more than a shared bloodline and DNA. There's a rainbow flowing between us. There's more of Matthew, more of Marilla even, in me than he could ever have accounted for.

The way he looks at me, I can tell he knows. He adds another *shit* under his breath before he stands. He holds out his hands in front of him and stares at me in the mirror. "Be honest with yourself. This can't be what you came for. A seedy gay bar and a dragged-out deadbeat daddy."

He's a harder sell than I feared. But I've come too far to give up so easily. "I'll get a job. I'm not afraid of hard work. I just need some time and a place. For a little bit. I'll be eighteen soon enough."

Matthew uncaps a tube of lipstick, considers the colour, and puts it back down on the table. "Grab that chair and sit like I told you to. You can put my stuff on

the floor."

I hurry to grab the chair. There's a bag, a lot like mine, flung open on the seat, even the thick floral-patterned material is almost the same. A cell phone, a roll of duct tape, a wig turned inside out, and several pairs of flesh-coloured tights sit on the surface, covering up what's underneath. Something sparkles from inside the bag as I pick it up. Hoping to see something glittery like sequins, I peer inside. The only thing remotely shiny are those big safety pins with the plastic tops meant for babies' diapers. Not exactly glamorous.

I glance at Matthew, who is absorbed in beating a powder puff against his face and cursing his crow's feet. The temptation to rummage through his private belongings and see what's filled his bag, his life, in the same way I rifled through his social media is so tempting. I don't think I can get away with it though. I move the bag roughly, hoping to uncover something more about my father. I wonder what secrets he has in there, what magic, what tools of transformation. With my knee, I bump the bag as I lift it, hoping to see more. The contents on top rearrange, the diaper pins jumping to the surface, and his phone's screen lights up. Behind the time and incoming message notification, the wallpaper is grainy and slightly distorted like someone used the phone to take a picture of a photograph. It's a younger Matthew as Marilla, face not as full, posing with what at first appears to be a bouquet of red roses in his arms. But the notification bars block my view. Maybe what I thought were roses aren't and that flash of red is not a flower bud but a blaze of hair. Even more curious to know what else is buried inside the bag, I stare at the phone's screen until it goes dark. I glance again at Matthew, who has finished beating his face, then place his carpetbag on the floor right next to my own.

"I really shouldn't let you stay," he says, waving his hand in front of him to help clear the dust cloud he created with the puff. "I don't have the room. I'm a mess. My life is a mess. One night. Just long enough for me to arrange to send you back to wherever it is you came from."

I came from you, I think. *I've come back to my point of origin.*

As I turn, I catch sight of myself in the panes of Matthew's folding mirror. Three of me look back. Three flabby bulges around my waistline, six boobs, six pit stains. I glance at Matthew, my hair and freckles reflecting back at me from under his makeup and wig. We're funhouse mirror variations of one another. Distorted and warped. Superimposed. Father and son. We're supposed to be a family.

I knew coming here that I probably wasn't going to be what Matthew thought his son should be. I anticipated that and knew I'd have to sell myself, a product no one has ever really wanted, including, it's become clear, my own father. But if I'm honest with myself, like Matthew told me to be, never did I stop to worry he wouldn't be what I had hoped. The father I'd been missing my entire life. A family that I'd lost, now recovered in this person.

None of this is turning out how I'd imagined. So I don't know what happens next.

All I know for sure as the six sets of eyes stare at me through the mirrored glass—three mine and three his—Matthew certainly isn't what I expected either, never mind what I thought he should be. But here we are, future and past on either side of us like train tracks going in separate directions, stuck, the two of us left behind at an empty station.

"Shit."

Glitterature writer **Paul Coccia** is the author of *Cub, The Player, I Got You Babe, Leon Levels Up,* and *On The Line* (co-authored with Eric Walters). Paul has a Master's of Fine Arts in Creative Writing from the University of British Columbia. You can often find him baking in his Toronto kitchen with his three dogs, nephew, and a parrot who loves spaghetti and French fries. Follow him @pauljcoccia on Instagram and Twitter.

NATASHA DEEN

4624463

A number by any other name...

For the Anne in all of us.

"A Library from The Days of Strife Unearthed"

CRAS, CAMPANA — Excavation teams uncovered one of the lost libraries from The Days of Strife. Under the guidance of Professor Karter Morgan, the site will be declared a historical location. Books and artifacts from the building will be housed in the Campana Museum of History.

"It's important to revere those who came before us," Minister Len said about the find. "Even as society evolves beyond our primitive origins, we must honour our history, so we never repeat past mistakes."

"**D**id you hear?" Diana's voice cut through the noise of kids at their lockers, getting their books before the first bell rang.

"I hear a lot of things," I said.

"The Minister is here," she whispered. "Someone spotted her coming out of the office."

I moved through the crowd to get to my locker. Lucky number three. Then I concentrated on the numbers of the combination: 46-24-46.

4-6-2-4-4-6. Plus 3 on the end. Numbers to live by.

91

Panicked whispers surged as word of the Minister's arrival spread. Not that any student or teacher at Cras Academy would admit to panic.

Pretending we didn't feel the feelings, however, didn't mean they didn't exist. The sour smell of adrenaline and cortisol permeated the air.

The panic was understandable. Minister Len only arrived when someone's violation of the rules of law was so egregious they risked enrolment in the Rehabilitation Centre.

That had only happened once in Cras Academy's history. Three years ago. That kid had dodged the Rehabilitation Centre, but barely. Luckier than the other kid, the one from Yunning Academy. They'd gone into the center. The whisper network said they'd never come out.

The Minister and her assistant came into view. Kids rippled away, their voices muted by fear. Soon, the only sound in the corridor was the click of the Minister's boots and almost-muted footfalls of her most trusted assistant, Gilbert.

Tall, broad-shouldered Gilbert, whose name was once a sigh on my lips and a whisper on the breeze. Gilbert, whose hand I thought I'd hold forever, until we'd been caught. In a society that had outlawed emotions—especially love—being a couple could have meant prison, the Rehabilitation Centre, prohibition from attending university, or worse. Rumours of a secret force that quietly erased troublesome citizens had always circulated. Those rumours were growing louder. So, too, were the murmur-

ings of a rising rebel force.

When we had stood in front of the Minister back then, Gilbert made his choice and I made mine. His landed him a placement with the Minister. I'd been sent to the President, a move the Minister has never forgiven, nor forgotten.

I watched Gilbert move through the hallway, daring him to make eye contact. I wasn't easy to miss. Tall brown-skinned girls with red hair and brown eyes were a minority, even in a world where genetic individuality was prized.

Gilbert walked past me as though I didn't exist. As though I'd never meant anything to him, at all. The ventilation system—or was it my imagination?—brought the faint scent of him to me. Ocean mist and thunderstorms. Memories of him, of us, flashed vividly in my mind. The warmth of his mouth. The strength of his touch. Cinnamon and spice coated the memories and left their lingering flavour on my tongue.

4-6-2-4-4-6-3. Numbers to die for.

I swallowed my longing and felt my body tremble in response.

Diana reached for my hand, then caught herself. "Something bad is going to happen."

We lived in a world where emotions were punished, families were outlawed, friendships were alliances of intellect and convenience, love and joy were stamped out, and I lived with a broken heart.

Something bad had already happened.

"We're in for a special treat today." Administrator Lynde's voice reverberated from the speakers at the front of the gym. Her fingers gripped the edges of the podium. "The Minister is here to bolster our spirits, to remind us of the philosophies and loyalties that unite us and to keep the eternal peace."

Her words were sweet spun cotton candy as they left her lips. Sugary pink words that changed colour when they whispered against my skin, and left behind the taste of bitter almonds.

Well-oiled springs and thick cushioning prevented any sounds of creaking chairs or shifting bodies. In my periphery were restless students. Indigo uniforms set against the silver chairs and white walls.

"My children"—Minister Len stood and took the spotlight and the microphone—"when I took office, my mandate was simple. That everywhere I went, I would bring comfort to the people. I would be visible to ensure the cohesion of our community." Her bright eyes swept over the audience, pausing briefly as if to take the measure of each person. "I know there is no one in this auditorium who fears me today. You are all loyal citizens."

Diana sagged in relief. I gently elbowed her.

"Long ago, our world struggled to find peace and prosperity," the Minister continued. "Our ancestors were well intentioned but mistaken. They created a society built on emotion, imagination, and dreams. A society

built on love."

I caught a couple of kids staring at me, waiting for my reaction. Who could blame them? I was the girl who'd been seduced by all of those things and had almost paid the ultimate price. The kids didn't look away, but unwilling to be their entertainment for the day, I stared them down. Exaggerating every movement, I mouthed, *Curiosity is an emotion.* Then I mimed a drill screwing into my skull. *Rehabilitation Centre.*

The kids jerked back to watching the Minister so fast they risked whiplash.

"What did their efforts gain anyone? Love is a lie, a seductive emotion that brings with it only greed, corruption, and disunity." Minister Len's voice rose with each word. She then retraced her steps and came to a stop next to Gilbert. And my treacherous body couldn't resist the urge to watch him. I drank him in, consuming every detail like raspberry cordial. The way the stage lights played along the planes and angles of his chin and jaw, how the shadows clung to the spot just below his cheekbones. My body went weightless. It remembered that spot, the sharp feel of his bones against my fingers. It remembered all his spots—the dimple on his left cheek when he smiled, the square shape of his nails, the soft tips of his fingers, the way he'd sigh when my arms went around his waist.

I fought the upsurge of emotions, cursing the ancestors for outlawing feelings because it meant none of us knew how to deal with them. A rush of chemicals and

hormones left me broken, as though the ocean had battered against the red cliffs unique to my homeland.

I wanted to storm the stage, to take Gilbert's hands in mine, to whisper: "the future doesn't matter, the past is forgotten," and then run away with him, to a place where our love was seen for the truth it was.

"The family structure *sounds* good, but what was its result?" Minister Len held the microphone close. Her voice reverberated from the speakers. "Divided loyalties, people violating the law in favour of those they called parents, siblings, or their surrogate family."

What was this feeling surging through me? Had the ancestors ever named this combination of rage, contempt, and helplessness? Did it leave them shaking and breath-less—did it prick their eyes with tears the same way it did to mine? I was certain they'd done more than name the feelings, that they'd taught their children how to ride these emotions, to harness them like crashing waves and use the chaos for power.

"We cannot fault our ancestors for dreaming, for thinking love was the ultimate expression of the human experience." The Minister continued to speak.

Beside me, Diana squeezed the hem of her tunic between her fingers.

Minister Len spread her hands wide. "But the proof of humanity's greatness is not in our emotion, but in our reason. Our logic. In the years since the End War, we have accomplished much." She paced across the stage and I lost my view of Gilbert.

Without the welcome distraction of Gilbert, I refocused all my attention on Minister Len. "You. Children born of science, raised by the collective, with no parents to perpetuate ignorance, nor siblings to create rivalry. Here, in the bosom of this academy, you are free to achieve your potential and to use it to better our world."

"Yet we must remain vigilant," she said, "for the frailties of the human body are many. Its desires and hungers can drive us to disastrous choices. We remember that dark day when a student violated our sacred rules."

Eyes shifted my way. Including Gilbert's. Unlike everyone else, who soon broke their stares, Gilbert didn't look away.

I met his challenge, then pressed my lips into a thin line at his small, answering smirk.

"You have heard that Professor Morgan's team has unearthed a library," said the Minister. "Despite the bombing that left it buried for over one hundred years, the building and its shelves are in good condition. I am here today to bestow a great honour on one of you."

I was still looking at Gilbert, but memory spun me back in time, under the canopy of night, when his lips first touched mine, and the way the sky lit up in ribbons of green and purple, as though heaven itself celebrated our love.

Minister Len flicked her fingers. The auditorium's lights rose.

Her gaze searched the auditorium and locked on me. An enigmatic smile twisted her lips. "Anne Shirley. You have come a long way from the girl who chose chaos and emotions over reason. Please join Gilbert. You two are to be part of the professor's team."

It was then that I understood her smile, then that the words shifted from the savoury spice of a congratulations to the sour twist of an ambush. Minister Len wasn't rewarding me. This was a punishment for my desecration of Cras's values and for escaping her attempt to put me in the Rehabilitation Centre. I was now to enter the room of the ancestors' knowledge and dreams. Close enough to touch their words but kept from reading them.

Gilbert moved down the steps, his footfall light.

It had been easy to look at him when I was safely hidden in the audience. But when he stood next to me, I struggled to keep from staring. Time had thickened his chest and sculpted his jawline. His dark hair was still a mass of tangles, but there was an order and structure to them. Like their master, they were no longer untamed, wild, or free.

He met my gaze. There was no warmth, no humour, no mischief in his eyes. I remember when they were as deep and infinite as the night sky, when looking into them felt like looking into my destiny. But that Gilbert no longer existed. His dark eyes were now vacant. Barren ground where nothing grew anymore. While I had expected to see some change, the reality of who he'd become was jarring. Then again, he'd avoided being sent to the Rehabilitation Centre by turning me in as a traitor to our society's morals. He got what he'd craved the most:

access to the Minister.

Gilbert pivoted, then strode to the exit. My feet stuttered on the polished wood floor as I rushed to keep up. Part of me wanted to follow in his footsteps with the same casual disregard he exuded. But my steps faltered, caught in the past and the present, in the dip and swoon of the way his shoulders moved in rhythm with his hips.

I followed in his wake. The boy for whom I had broken all the rules. The boy who had broken me.

On the light spectrum, white is a combination of all the colours. The administrators felt this was the best representation of all that the school had to offer. Thus, every academy room was the same: white walls, white ceilings, white padded chairs nestled under white desks. All on white floors that shone like glass. The classroom we now approached was empty, but that didn't mean we were alone. Guards patrolled the halls, at regular and irregular intervals. The school administration said it was for security. I marvelled at how easily their lies slipped from their mouths.

"The star student," Gilbert said as we entered the room. "I'm not surprised."

"I've learned everything the teachers put before me and more," I said.

He leaned back. "And has the knowledge changed you? Finally made you a citizen worthy of the Minister's

cabinet?"

"Like you?" I sat at one of the desks. "You're the talk of the school. The Minister's favourite."

"Someone had to be," Gilbert said, still standing. "We knew it could never be you."

"I'm sure you've served her well," I said, for the benefit of anyone listening as they passed by.

The edges of his lips curled. Not quite a smile. "I do what's necessary for the benefit of my society."

"Even if it means betraying a friend?"

"We were never friends, Anne."

His words washed over me in shades of yellow and green, until I could taste the sweet bitterness of each syllable.

"You'll come with me tomorrow to the archive building. We'll sort the books, per Professor Morgan's instructions." The edges of his lips lifted again. "You always wanted to be near the old stories."

The memories—pretending we were nothing to each other during the day, the two of us sneaking to the garden in the cool of the evening. Him, whispering that he knew what love was, and his heart belonged to me. All our shared plans and secret schemes. "Don't—don't bring our past into this," I said. "Not now."

He put his hands on my desk and leaned so far forward I could feel the heat emanating from his skin. "The last few years—"

A sudden click of the door knob startled us both. We looked up as the door swung open.

The timing was impeccable. I had no doubt that the person on the other side of the door had been listening to every word we'd said.

The Minister took off her gloves, pulling each finger loose, until she slid them off her hand. "How old are you now, Anne?"

"Eighteen, ma'am."

Away from the stage lights, the faint lines along the sides of her mouth were visible. She hadn't had them the last time I had seen her. Back then, she hadn't had laugh lines. She still didn't.

"It's been some time since we've seen each other."

"Three years, ma'am."

"Ma'am. Time has taught you manners." She watched me, letting the moment linger, surveying my face to see if there was any sarcasm in use of the title. She traced the scar along her palm. "I still remember our last meeting." Her eyes hardened. "Quite the little defender of books and feelings, weren't you?"

I kept my hands on my lap, my shoulders straight. "I never attacked you, ma'am. You had the knife. Your hand slipped."

She massaged the scar. "The tribunal agreed with your version of events. I wanted you in the Rehabilitation Centre. They wanted you housed in a temporary adoption."

"I was young. They knew I didn't warrant the centre."

"Indeed," she said. "You were an exceptional student. The adjudicators didn't want to lose that, did they? You—you were their shining star, the epitome of what a logical upbringing could yield." She leaned close, as if proximity would reveal my secrets to her searching gaze. "What happened, Anne? How did a child who once spouted every virtue of our society devolve into such an embarrassment? What could have possibly broken your loyalty to our state?"

I remained silent and stayed focused on her.

"I told them there could only be one reason."

"Yes, ma'am?" I asked and delighted in the steadiness of the question.

"I told them something must have gone wrong when the scientists put you together in the lab. A mistake in how they mixed your DNA. But no one wanted to admit to such a mistake. No one wanted to acknowledge that academics couldn't prevent an unbalanced citizen from choosing emotion over reason." Her teeth flashed in a feral smile. "Special treatment for a special girl."

"Temporary adoptions are an accepted method of therapy given to many children deemed to be of worth to our community. I am equally as special as thousands of other children." I inclined my head. "Ma'am."

"Hmm." Her gaze flicked to Gilbert. "How did you find your time under my tutelage?"

"Eye-opening, Ma'am."

If Gilbert's back went any straighter, he would crack

his vertebrae.

"And in comparison to what you've heard of the President's manner?" she asked.

"There's no comparison," he said.

She waited, but he didn't elaborate.

The Minister grunted, then turned back to me. "The headmistress says you've excelled in your studies, Anne, and there have been no more...mistakes." Her gaze flicked between us. "Our society values its loyal citizens but prizes its citizens who have been redeemed. You and Gilbert. Two errant children, blinded by their juvenile emotions, now basking in the light and purity of logic and reason."

She heaved herself out of the chair. "Don't make a mockery of this opportunity," she said as she walked out the door.

Gilbert's voice dropped low. "Can you do what is asked of you?"

"I know my job and I'll do it," I told him. "Just make sure you do yours."

The crowds had gathered outside to view the procession of the books into the archive. I watched from the front row, waiting for my signal to go inside.

When the last of the procession had climbed the carpeted steps and walked through the etched glass doors, the guards at the entrance nodded for me to proceed. I stepped forward, alongside Gilbert, and preceded him into the building. As I moved through the doors, I noticed the fresh paint on the walls. At a distance, I hadn't been able to see the graffiti that it covered. This close, I saw the words underneath. Red text seeping through the white walls like a wound that refused to heal: *Love is Love* and *Emotions are Natural*.

Two rows of pillars bracketed the marble entryway. The wide space was empty, save for the dark lacquered desk in the centre and the white-haired man behind it.

He rose as we approached. "The department for the historical books is here, on the main floor." He pointed to the spot on the map. "You need to present your identification when you arrive and leave." The guard turned a gold-leaf book toward us. "During the day, you must wear one of our uniforms. You change in the locker room."

I did as I was told and emerged from the room, clad in a slim-fit white jumpsuit with booties. There were no pockets or compartments in which a person could hide a book. The arms also ended in gloves, ensuring no one could hide pages in their sleeves.

"Are you sure you can handle this?" Gilbert asked as he came up to me.

I didn't answer because I didn't have one. The urge to clutch the books close and run away overwhelmed me. So did the desire to shove them into the hands of my fellow citizens and say, "They're lying! There is no danger in books! There is no harm in love."

The team assembled, and the guard led us down a series of hallways and through three sets of doors, each of

them guarded by a sentry.

"Here we are." The guard stopped in front of a set of metal doors that were slightly ajar. He stepped forward and pushed them open.

A thick shaft of sunlight streamed through the opening, temporarily blinding me. I raised my hands against the light and squinted to see what was there. Dust motes danced on the yellow beams. The scent of paper and dust wafted by me.

"You'll need these." Someone came through the doorway.

Karter. It had been a year since I'd seen them. They wore a mask, leaving only their blue eyes and olive forehead visible. "Anne."

It was the only acknowledgment I would receive of our previous contact. I took the hint. "Karter."

Karter's brief nod at Gilbert barely acknowledged his presence.

"This way." Without waiting to see if we followed, they walked away.

I glanced at the guard, decided remaining on the periphery of their awareness was best, and caught up to Karter.

The space had floor-to-ceiling windows that looked onto the courtyard. Four open skylights, lining the glass ceiling, let in the breeze. Inside the centre stood a bin, filled to the top with books. Spiralling out in a starfish pattern stood additional bins. Beside them, people were sorting the books into precise columns and rows.

"You will be the first line of reviewers," Karter said, leading us to the centre bin. "Take a book"—they demonstrated—"and note the cover and title. Flip it over, then read the story synopsis. That'll be on the inside of the dust jacket or on the back of the book. From there, you sort it into one of two piles. Fiction or non-fiction. Then you sort what the genre is. For fiction, is it romance, thriller, mystery? For non-fiction, what is the focus? Science? History?" Karter nodded at the various bins branching out. "They're labelled. You take the book there, then the secondary crew will take over. Got it?"

I nodded.

Gilbert moved to the bin and began his work with the disinterested air of a person with a day of sorting ahead of them. I moved at a slower pace. Tentatively, I took out a book. Dust coated the cover. I wiped the surface. What had the world been like—really been like—when love, family, and friendship were considered character values and not deficits?

"Anne, you seem unfocused." Karter came to a stop beside me.

"I was thinking of history," I said. "Of our elders and ancestors." I thought about this for a moment, then continued.

"What brutal lives they must have led. You're born, then told that by virtue of birth, the people in your home were defined as family and you owed them loyalty and love. Then they transferred that to the corporation and made business a surrogate family. What horror."

"Our way is much more civilized and humane," Karter said. "Children born of surrogates, raised in the academy. Occasionally housed in different adoptive placements. None of these 'I feel' or non-scientific reasonings to bias people against each other. No economic disparity to create social classes." Karter put a gentle hand on my shoulder. "It's romantic, to think of love conquering all, to think of these idealized notions of family and friendship. But if we don't belong to anyone, then we belong to everyone. And if we don't belong anywhere, we belong everywhere. A global community is the right way to build a society."

Karter left and I returned my attention to the book. The picture on the cover was of a man holding a woman's hand. Her face was full of a devotion I knew too well, a devotion I tried to forget. She looked at him the way I'd once looked at Gilbert.

Flipping the cover, I read the back.

Fractured families, betrayed alliances, war, death, and doomed love. Everything my society warned us about the ancient times. *And yet...* and yet, the idea of love was a melody that sang inside of me, a sliver of light and colour in a world of grey.

"You're taking too long," said Gilbert. "You're to review them, not read them."

I gave him a sharp salute, trekked the book to its next bin, and returned to repeat the process. The day soon fell into a quiet rhythm. Overhead, the sunshine gave way to clouds and a soft pattering of rain on the skylights.

"Should we close the skylights?" I asked Karter.

"Someone will get to that," they said.

But it took an hour for someone to come. By then, errant raindrops had made their mark on some of the books.

When the group broke for lunch, I took a spot away from everyone else.

"Do you remember when the matron caught you writing a poem about apples?" Gilbert sat beside me. He'd pushed the hood off his hair.

"Who could forget?" Matron had stopped lunch and dragged me to the front of the cafeteria. My body still burned with humiliation when I remembered how she berated me for my emotional response to an apple. Her words felt like a toxic heat: *Poetry! It's the very heart of what went wrong in the ancient times! Food is to be eaten, its sustenance appreciated. We do not engage emotionally with our food. We do not imbue it with characteristics and values it does not possess.* She ushered me to the office and asked if it was the first time I'd given into my emotions. I'd lied and told her yes.

Then she'd brought in Gilbert.

He'd told her everything—our secret meetings, how he'd gotten me to confess my love for him. Then he handed her a book, a story I'd written for him.

After Matron read the dedication, *For Gilbert, with all of my love*, she burned it in front of everyone, then

submitted the paperwork to have me admitted to rehabilitation.

But my grades had given the Ministry pause. My previous devotion to the cause had given them second thoughts. A phone call later and I was processed as a temporary adoption with the President. Gilbert was placed in the neighbouring house, with the Vice-President, Matthew. That was three years ago. Since then, I've never written another stanza of poetry, never put any story on the page again, and I don't look at apples the same way.

Gilbert coiled his finger around a strand of my hair, tugged it. "I've never looked at apples the same way since." He leaned in and whispered, "They tasted different after I read your poem. Sweeter." He leaned back. "It is wrong to have favourite fruits and colours. All things are equal. But if I were back in ancient times, I think red would have been my favourite colour." He released the lock of hair.

I took a deep breath, then tried to finish my lunch. But my fingers wouldn't stop shaking. Neither would my insides. In the end, I held my cup, so that if anyone looked over, my body would seem steady.

A little before the day finished, I came across a book whose genre seemed muddled. Its title, *Block 2119,* gave no hint to what it was about. The cover was equally indecipherable: an apartment building, with silhouettes in the window. A perusal of the dust jacket didn't help. It could have been mystery, but maybe romance?

I flipped open the book and scanned the first page. Then the second. The words were hypnotic. Black text on the page drew me into another world, where the main character worried and laughed, where she revelled in the touch of her girlfriend's arm around her waist.

Someone snatched the book from my grip.

"You're to sort, not read," said Karter. "I could get fired if someone caught you."

"I wasn't reading," I said. "I was trying to sort it."

"Next time"—Karter held the book tightly—"ask me."

"What does it matter? The books will be put on display for people to read."

"Adults," Karter corrected.

"But I'm eighteen, an adult."

Karter shook their head. "You're still in school. Your eighteen doesn't count. Not yet."

"Fine." I pulled at the uniform's collar, trying to get air into the suit. "You read it and tell me."

They balked. "Oh—"

Then they glanced over their shoulder. "I'm sure general fiction will work for this one. Bin it, please."

I took my time ferrying the book to its bin, measuring each step with my thoughts. "Here you are." I handed it to the lady at the general fiction bin. "So, what happens next? To the books?"

"They're taken to sanitation, where dirt is removed and any torn pages or bindings are fixed," she said. "Then they're archived until it's time to put them out for display."

"Do you get to read them before they're archived or moved for lending?"

She laughed, a thin sound that thickened into a question in my mind.

"Oh, no," she said. "That would be favouritism. No one person before the other."

I nodded, then went back to sorting. By the end of the day, my feet hurt and so did my back. I stretched, scanning the glass ceiling and the thick metal lattice that held the panes in place. I detoured under the skylights as I left for the day, and tracked the small pools of water collecting under them.

Before I went to the locker, the question still ringing in my ears, I headed to the reception desk. The man who'd signed me in was still there.

"Do you know which of the previously archived books are the most popular with readers?" I asked.

He frowned. "I wouldn't have access to that information."

My question grew as did my need to solve the puzzle. "I thought all databases were centralized?" I counted the columns on the left. "I suppose your archives don't need to be synced with the other departments."

"Of course they do," he said. "We're equally important."

I waited for a beat. The question was still there, but an answer was forming. The confirmation of a rumour I'd heard. "Then you have the information."

His face went red. "What I meant is that I can't access

that information for you."

I nodded, then went to the change room.

Karter found me as I was tying my sneakers. Taking a spot beside me on the bench, they said, "You worked hard today. I'm not going to mention your slip up with that book." As they placed their hands on their knees, the sleeves of their tunic slid up.

I caught the flash of black text on their wrist. "My... slip up."

They licked their lips. "Yes, there's no need for us to talk about it." Karter pulled down their sleeves.

I pivoted to face them. "Once I'm eligible to sign out the books, how do I do it?"

Karter stilled, then gave a slow nod, as if they knew what I was asking and sought to give me an answer that wouldn't get them in trouble. "The receptionist out front would take your name. If you're deemed worthy and a contributing member of society, you are granted access."

"Are those records public? Can I see who's signed out the books before me?"

Karter's smile was small. "I don't know that anyone wants to track who read the books before they have."

"What if I want to discuss it with someone?"

"You don't!" Karter caught themselves. "That is—you would talk to someone here, in the building. Someone who works with the books, who can speak to the nuance and danger the text presents." An employee came into the locker room, and Karter stood. "Look, Anne, being accepted to read the ancestors' works is one of the highest honours our society gives. It's incredibly hard to meet that standard. You have a history. The chances they will allow you into the upper levels are low."

I pointed at their wrist. "The ink will always be fading, but never faded. That's how the rehabilitation centres work. Our transgressions are never fully erased. But if they let you work here, then maybe I get to read the books. You said I would talk to someone—"

Karter moved to my locker and handed me my satchel. "You're obviously tired and misunderstand my instructions. Have a good night."

I took the bag from them, slung it across my torso. Karter and I moved at the same time, banging into each other.

"I apologize," they said. "Go ahead."

This time, a woman sat behind the receptionist's desk. "I'll need to see your ID when you sign out."

I dug into my bag, then dug deeper. *Karter.* "It must have fallen out at the locker. I'll be back."

When I turned the corner of the hallway, I saw Karter at the end, waiting. They spotted me and disappeared around an adjacent corridor.

I hurried after them, spun left. Karter stopped at a doorway, gave me a long look, then stepped inside. I rushed to catch up. The carpet muffled the sounds of my footfalls. The door was closed, with only a sliver of space visible. I peered through the crack, but saw only movements of bodies, and nothing identifiable.

"—went well." I recognized the Minister's voice. "Do

you think either of them would be acceptable to move into the role after graduation?"

"The boy, perhaps," said Karter. "The girl would prove…problematic at the later stages."

"Why do you say that?" A new voice, bass.

"You don't know?" Karter, again. "That's Anne Shirley."

"That's the kid?" said Bass-Voice. "I thought she had blonde hair."

"Grew into red," said Karter. "Genetics, right?"

"She made the news with that stunt. If we could get her to sign on to this department…think of what it would mean. She could be a beacon, a triumph of reason over emotion. Have you seen the graffiti? The government is doing its best, but these people spray-painting that logic is a lie and love is truth…If we get Anne in this department, maybe those rumblings stop. The girl who wrote poetry, now guarding the books of the ancients."

I tensed in the silence.

"—Karter, take her under your wing. See if you can get her onside. In the meantime—" the Minister's voice drew closer.

"I'm due for leave in a couple of weeks, ma'am," said Karter.

"Do what you can," she said.

I scuttled to the room opposite, closed the door, and waited in the dark. A second later, the other door squeaked open. Another second, the rolling sound of a heavy container on wheels.

I watched them emerge—Karter, a man, and Minister

Len. Karter pushed a bin of books.

"I'll get started on these," Karter said.

"Want help?" The two others paused.

"To throw books into a furnace? I can handle it."
Karter moved off to fulfill the task. Quiet closed around
me. I had the information. The puzzle pieces were falling
into place, and the answers were coming to me. But a new
question emerged. What would I do with the knowledge
I'd gained?

"You must have misheard," Diana said when I returned
to the academy.

We stood on the bank of the pond, alone save the
evening breeze and the lingering scent of the rain.

"I heard perfectly. The rumours are true. They're
burning the books." I told her about the skylight leaking
water. "No one fixes it because the books will be
destroyed. And no one would answer my questions about
who reads the ancestors' works because no one is allowed."

"They have books on display."

"*Some of them.* Behind glass," I said. "Where no one
can touch them." I reached into my bag and pulled out
the copy of *Block 2119*.

Diana hissed, "You stole the book?"

I shook my head. "Karter dropped it when they were
taking the books to the furnace. I think they meant for
me to find it."

"Why would someone who just met you suddenly take you into their confidence about burning books?"

I didn't answer. The truth would only complicate matters between us.

Diana's restless stride took her away, then back. "You'll get caught. It's a trap."

"It doesn't matter. What they're doing is wrong. They tell us they're holding the ancient ways sacred, but it's a lie. They're destroying our past, Diana, and there can be no future unless we understand our past."

"When they catch you, they'll think I helped." She faced me, her eyes as dark as the water. "We'll both end up in the Rehabilitation Centre."

There was rustling in the trees behind us. I dropped my voice. "There are bigger things at stake."

"I don't want to end up in the centre," Diana said.

"You won't." I took her hands. Night and worry had turned her fingers ice-cold. "Stick to your part of the plan, and nothing will go wrong."

The night I put my plan into action, I wandered the downtown streets until it grew dark, then darker still. Deep in the alleys, where dark recesses gave rise to shadowed thoughts, I traced my fingers along the painted vandalism and felt the kinship between myself and those who'd painted the words.

Dare to Dream

IMAGINATION IS BEAUTIFUL
NOT AFRAID TO LOVE
IT'S OKAY TO BE SCARED.

The lettering was still wet. Paint dripped down the walls, pooled along my fingers, and stained my skin red.

The graffiti had begun a year and a half ago, with small tags and the occasional sticker. But it was growing. The tags were getting larger, the images more ornate. What had begun as someone's personal rebellion was dangerously close to becoming a cause.

At the appointed time, I headed back to the Ministry of Books. Toward the end of our ancestors' reign, deepfake technology and video surveillance were no longer used. These days, security people patrolled the sidewalks and guarded the entrances to all buildings.

I went into the alley, to the small bag I'd hidden behind one of the garbage bins. I pulled on the camouflage suit and hid my hair under the hood. Then I climbed the outside fire escape to the roof.

Security was solely focused on ground-level access to the building because no one thought that someone would try to get in through the roof, where a glass ceiling with skylights and a twenty-foot free fall to the ground made for a challenging break-in.

And that was their mistake. A person could only get so far on a thought. Imagination would always take them much further. And I was an imaginative intruder with an unconventional plan. Spreading out my body weight, lying flat, I inched my way to the broken skylight.

A pen knife and patience helped me break in where the seal was loose. It was a tight fit, but I could wriggle in.

I pulled out a grappling rope, hooked it on the frame, and tested the hold. Good enough. Before I dropped it into the room, I looped three candles—extra long, extra wide—near the grapple. High enough to prevent disaster, low enough to cause a commotion. The strike of a match and they were lit.

While the flame burned, I dropped the rope, scuttled off the roof, and raced down the stairs, heading for the main entrance. My timing was almost perfect. Just as I reached the corner, the fire alarm went off. Shouting ensued.

The security guards ran inside and were so focused on the alarm they didn't notice me trailing behind them. Out of breath, I ducked behind a pillar. As the guards raced to the reception desk, I sprinted to the next pillar. Then the next. Five pillars, five chances to reach the end of the hallway.

The evening lights cast enough shadows for me to get lost in them, to move to the furnace room without detection. I paused outside the doors. On the other side, there was no hum of boilers, no quiet roar of fire. Aware there might be someone on the other side, I stepped through.

The room was as dark as the hallway. I didn't bother searching for the lights. If everything went according to plan, the space would be illuminated soon enough. I didn't have to wait long.

The lights flipped on, blinding me, not that I needed sight. I knew who was at the switch.

"Anne," said the Minister. "I'm disappointed, but not surprised."

Diana stepped out from behind her. "I'm sorry, Anne. I couldn't be blamed for what you were doing."

Minister Len put her hand on Diana's shoulder.

Diana shrank under her grip.

"How could you pull this poor girl into your deceit?" asked the Minister.

"I didn't want to report you," said Diana, "but I had to do what was necessary."

"Yes," said the Minister, "Diana has shown her true allegiance." The Minister's gaze turned to me. "So have you."

"What now?" I jerked my thumb at the books in the bin and willed my body to stay relaxed, but I was certain they could hear the thump of my heart. "Another tribunal?"

"How could you be so foolish?" The Minster moved close to peer up at me. "You were so close to graduating. You had turned your life around." Her eyes narrowed. "Now, this…rash move. What could you possibly have hoped to accomplish?"

I waited for her to put it together.

"Ah." Clarity bloomed across her face. "You're aiming for another tribunal, aren't you? A chance to bring yourself into the spotlight once more. To what end? You think people will follow your—" Her mockery gave way to another bloom. "*You're* the one behind the graffiti, aren't you?"

"Minister, I'm in the academy. How could I possibly have time to move through the city—"

"You found time to break into the archives, didn't you?" She straightened, then massaged her scar. "You won't accomplish your goals. I have full authority over repeat offenders. There will be no moment for you to corrupt anyone. The papers to send you to the Rehabilitation Centre will be signed within the hour."

Diana widened her stance, put her hands behind her back, and nodded.

"Excellent resolve," Minister Len said to her. "We must always be accountable to the consequences of our decisions." Turning to me, she continued, "I think you know what this means for you, Anne."

I did. *4-6-2-4-4-6-3.* Numbers to scheme by.

The Minister smiled.

I wondered if she was heady with delight, if the knowledge of what she was doing to me made her blood quicken.

"Three years in the centre will smooth any of your edges," she said. "If they don't kill you first."

She moved to the exit.

"This society will never survive, not with its current philosophy," I said.

The Minister arched an eyebrow.

"You said this society was built on reason and logic."

"It is."

"Before it could be built," I told her, "it had to be imagined. Someone—a lot of someones—had to daydream what a world built on logic would be like. Only then could they put their imagining into reality."

The Minister's smile froze, then flickered. "They didn't imagine. They thought."

"They dreamed. Where else does thought come from?"

Minister Len left, but I noticed her steps weren't as confident as before.

As the sound of her heels faded, Diana and I warily assessed each other, our ears cocked to the door. In the silence that followed, we held a silent vigil. I filled the quiet with memories of our shared laughter, our secrets, and all the endless conversations we had about the rebellion. And how terrified she was to ever be discovered.

Diana put her hand to her stomach and took a faltering breath. "Anne," she said. "What I did…" She collapsed against the wall.

Was this performance for me or for anyone on the other side of the doors? I watched her for a few seconds, listened for any sound in the hallway.

"Nice touch with the nod," I finally said.

Diana's eyes narrowed, then she laughed, the sound fragile, then gaining confidence.

Next time," she said, "*you* play the cowardly friend. I'm sorry—"

"Don't apologize," I said. I closed the distance and

gripped her fingers. "This was a frightening plan, and it could have gone horribly wrong, but, Diana, look at what you did. You're the reason we're as far as we are. We made a plan, and you did what you had to do." I glanced over her shoulder. "They're sure to pick you for this department, now."

She nodded. "I'll protect them, Anne. I'll protect all the books."

A bang down the hallway pulled our attention. Moments later, the President entered with Minister Len and Gilbert.

"Anne," said the President.

"Marilla."

She turned to the Minister. "Leave us. Gilbert, stay here, but watch the door."

The Minister opened her mouth, then snapped it shut when Marilla stared her down.

"Diana, you may go, with thanks for your service," said Marilla.

They left. Gilbert closed the door.

Marilla gripped me by the shoulders. "You foolish, foolish girl." She pulled me into her arms.

I sank into her embrace, the way I had all those years ago when she'd fostered me. Marilla was home. She always would be. Because that was what the founders of our society would never understand. No matter how they mixed genetics, no matter what we were taught, love was love, and it was woven into our DNA. It turned strangers into friends, and friends into family. "I love you. I've

missed you."

"You weren't supposed to trigger the next move until you had graduated," she said. "Though I appreciate it. My bones are too old to climb walls and spray messages."

"They're burning books, Marilla. I couldn't wait."

Her face tightened. She cupped my face, stared at me as if trying to memorize every pore. "They're going to send you to Kantan Rehabilitation Centre. It's the worst of all of them."

Gilbert took my hand. "It's going to be fine, Marilla. I'll be with Anne. We've planned and sacrificed for this for years. Anne was always meant to be the rebel." He smiled. "We both know her temper would never allow her to be the sycophant the Minister needed. Three years, we've worked. Three years, I've lied through my teeth and done the bidding of Minister Len. Now, she has chosen me, as her right hand, to accompany Anne and ensure she reaches the centre." He squeezed my fingers. "I've missed you. Every moment of every day."

I squeezed back. Gilbert. The boy for whom I had broken all the rules. The boy who broke me of my loyalty to a corrupt regime, who saved my heart and helped me save myself.

Marilla took a deep breath. "You're sure you've got everything in place?"

"While you, Diana, and Anne worked your side, I made contact with one of the lieutenants of the rebellion, Karter," said Gilbert. "They made contact with Anne, and they've set up the next steps. The coach carrying Anne and

me will have an accident," said Gilbert. "Karter's due for their time off. No one will miss them for weeks. Karter will meet us at the rendezvous point. We've memorized the code for the safe house. *4-6-2-4-4-6-3*."

Marilla clutched us close, then pushed us apart. "Find Matthew," she said. "Find my brother and bring him home."

Gilbert's fingers trailed along my arms until he reached my wrists. Then I felt cold metal encircle my skin, and looked down to see him gently locking a pair of manacles on me. "When transporting a prisoner, protocol dictates I keep your hands restrained. Only until we're in the coach, though. We just play the roles."

I nodded.

"Wait," Marilla called out. "What if it's not a numeric code?"

"Put it in your keycode," I told her.

She did.

"What does it spell?"

"*Imagine*," she said.

"Imagine," I repeated, "a world of love and friendship."

Gilbert led me down the hallway. He glanced around, pulled me into an empty room and closed the door. Then his body was pressed alongside mine, and I went light at the weight of him against me.

"Gilbert—" My attempt to push him away was half-hearted. My fingers lingered on the breadth of his chest, then rose to the smooth column of his neck. "This is too risky."

His deep laugh sent vibrations through me. "Says the girl who risked the Rehabilitation Centre twice." He threaded his fingers through my hair, leaned close to inhale its fragrance. "Anne," he whispered, and my skin prickled at the sound of my name on his lips. "My Anne."

I tilted my head, lifting my hands to cup his face. Late-evening stubble on his cheeks grazed my fingertips, and I put my lips to the sweet hollow of his neck, then his jawline, glorying in the rasp of his whiskers against my mouth.

"Anne." His whisper was no longer a whisper.

Three years. Three long years I'd missed the touch and strength of him, and now, memory and reality rushed through me in a roaring flame. The feel of his hair in my fingers, how solid his body was against mine, the way we fit so perfectly together, the warmth of his mouth.

The hunger for him blazed through me, until I wasn't certain if I was kissing him or devouring him. But I gathered the front of his shirt, pulled him close, and closer still, feeling the hammer of his heartbeat against my ribs. Nothing—not even iron shackles—was going to stop me from holding onto love.

The sound of a door closing in the distance pulled us apart.

Gilbert pulled away, his breathing hitching. "Next time," he smiled, "we take our time." He ran his finger along my bottom lip. "Until you, there was only imagination. Now, I don't have to imagine love," he said. "Not with you. Not ever."

I took his hand, pressed my lips against his fingers. "Now, we imagine together."

4-6-2-4-4-6-3. Numbers to change the world by.

Guyanese-Canadian **Natasha Deen** is a bestselling author and a recipient of the Queen Elizabeth II Platinum Jubilee Medal. Natasha's novels include *In the Key of Nira Ghani* (Amy Mathers Teen Book Award) and *Spooky Sleuths: The Ghost Tree* (*School Library Journal* Best Books of 2022). Her most recent YA title, *The Signs and Wonders of Tuna Rashad*, was a *Globe & Mail's* Top 100 Books for 2022. When she's not writing, she teaches Introduction to Children's Writing with the University of Toronto's SCS and spends an inordinate amount of time trying to convince her pets that she's the boss of the house. Visit Natasha at www.natashadeen.com.

DEIRDRE KESSLER

The Wooden Box

One look inside changes things forever.

This story is dedicated to John and Jennie Macneill.

Day One: May 15th

*T*hey have given me the room a chimney runs through, up narrow backstairs from the kitchen end of the house. The room is fusty; no one has used it in a long time. The only access is by the backstairs. When the Swans are asleep tonight, I will be able to descend the stairs and go outdoors without their knowing, as there's a door separating the back entrance and foyer from the kitchen.

When Hilda Swan brought me to this room, she put my case on the bed, opened the small east window, and said I should settle in before supper. She stood waiting for me to answer her. Words arose in me and climbed ladders, did somersaults, appeared and disappeared. A few words made it to my tongue. *Say it, Anne. Say* thank you. *Say anything.* I swallowed, and the words were gone.

Hilda Swan smiled at me. Such warmth in her smile. Then she left me alone.

But when all Space has been beheld
And all Dominion shown
The smallest Human Heart's extent
Reduces it to none.[1]

130

From the small window that faces east, I see the farm where my so-called twin once lived a long time ago. A larger window, in a dormer, faces south with a view of the front field and the red clay road to town. On the other side of the road is a woodland. That is where I shall go tonight when the Swans are sleeping.

I'll find mayflowers for you, Emily. It's May 15th. I begin anew the day you died.

If I don't find mayflowers, there will be another plant to pluck in remembrance. There are heaps of wild-strawberry flowers—*Fragaria virginiana*. And already I've seen leaves of the bluebead lily—*Clintonia borealis*—soon to have its delicate pale-yellow flowers, and in a few weeks there'll be clusters of blue beads. Oh, Emily, that blue makes my heart almost stop, just as some of your poems do.

Your poems and my drawing things are in my suitcase with my herbarium, which, thank Persephone, I was allowed to bring with me.

This is *my room*.

There's a dresser against the slanted north wall. The bed is against the west wall, the shared wall with what I suspect is the Swans' bedroom or a guest bedroom. Or a child's room. Did they have children? Why is there no door between this room and the rest of the upstairs of the house? Is this a room for a hired hand? Do other old farmhouses on the Island have upstairs rooms you can get to only by separate stairs?

Tomorrow morning, the sun from the little east window will strike my eyes and awaken me in *my room*.

I am grateful for a room of my own and grateful that at last an adoption was successful. The Swans are elderly; I will be able to help them around their farm. And I am very, very grateful to have this one faded photograph of Arabella, my mother, and Victor, my father. The director at the orphanage gave me the photograph this morning.

Arabella Grace Turner and Victor Davenport Milne.

Do you think I resemble them, Emily?

I do.

Yesterday morning, I was lurking outside the door of the orphanage office when I overheard the director telling the Swans that rumour had it that my mother had run off with a red-haired rogue and I was the flame-haired product of the pairing. The director said, "Here is the one thing remaining that belonged to the parents. It was left with Anne when she was brought to the orphanage. I didn't work here then. The accompanying letter instructed us to keep this for Anne and give it to her when she was eighteen years old. Luckily, the letter was in Anne's file. I had to search to find what her parents had left here."

I peered into the room to see what the director was giving to the Swans. A wooden box!

As I rushed into the room, the director was saying, "I opened the…" She halted mid-sentence.

Words gushed from the deep well in me and gathered on my tongue, crowded, elbowed one another, pushed and shoved to the tip of my tongue, to my lips: *What is in the box?*

I could not make words leave my body.

"Oh, yes—do come in, Anne," said the director. "These are the people we have been telling you about who have come to adopt you. Mr. and Mrs. Swan. Gordon and Hilda."

The director placed the wooden box on the desk.

"We are very happy to meet you, Anne," said Mrs. Swan.

"Yes, indeed," said Mr. Swan. "We hope you will like living on our farm with us. We hear you are a good student and you like animals and you have a talent for drawing."

"We'd like you to spend a couple of weeks or so with us," Mrs. Swan added, "so you can decide if you would like to live with us permanently."

I looked at them and smiled as best I could, but my euphoria over the wooden box overcame politeness, and I went to the director's desk and put my hands on the box. *My* box.

Oh, Mother and Father, thank you.

My hands trembled, and tears sprang unbidden into my eyes.

The director cleared her throat. "We thought you would like to have this photograph, Anne, of your parents."

She handed me a photograph.

I took the photograph. Time stopped. The air shimmered, and a sudden, deep silence surrounded me, and I was alone, the only person in the room.

Arabella Grace Turner and Victor Davenport Milne: my parents.

As I stared at the picture of my parents, their faces began to move, just for a second. And I could feel something at the back of my head and inside my head, a stirring that echoed quickly in my chest. My entire body began to vibrate. I was transfixed, as though I could enter the photograph and join my parents. We were three together again, a family, just the three of us, outside of time.

The director broke the spell.

"The Swans will hold onto the box for now, Anne."

I looked at her and then at the Swans.

Words gathered on my tongue, moved to the tip of my tongue, to my lips. *It is my box. I will take it now. It belongs to me. I want to open the box **now**.*

No words made it into the air as I held onto the photograph. The Swans carried the box and my suitcase to their car. The director said goodbye, I got into the car, and we drove away from the orphanage.

On the drive from the orphanage to the Swans' farm, Gordon Swan pointed out many landmarks. When we passed a luminous yellow pasture, an entire field shimmering with gold, Hilda Swan said, "Terrible how they've let that field get all overgrown with weeds. Dreadful weed, dandelion."

But I was a bumblebee, intoxicated, hypnotized,

transfixed by a universe of yellow flowers. Gordon Swan looked in the rear-view mirror and saw the delight in my face.

"I hear you're an aspiring botanist, Anne," he said. "Then you probably know what makes the sound *zzub, zzub, zzub.*"

I didn't know. I looked at his reflection in the rear-view mirror and shook my head.

"It's a bee flying backwards," he said.

"Oh, for goodness' sake, Gordon," said Hilda Swan. "The girl is fourteen, not four!"

I smiled and appreciated his cheerfulness. I feel no expectation from him to speak.

"Maybe you'd like to go with us to the Macphail Woods sometime," Gordon Swan said. "They've been growing native species in their nursery and woodlands."

We turned onto a clay road bowered by tall maple trees and poplar trees. Gordon Swan named all the people who lived on their road. A farm adjacent to theirs once belonged to the Cuthberts, whom Gordon Swan said long ago—when his grandparents were alive—had adopted a girl, who must have been my doppelganger as she was also named Anne and also had red hair. The Cuthberts' Anne could certainly speak.

What had the Swans been told about me? How did they find me? Why had they chosen me? Why hadn't the people at the orphanage told me about that box years ago? Why would I need to wait until I was eighteen to have it? If only I'd known about the box, I'd have found it years and years ago. I'm fourteen! If I'm mature enough to decide if I want to be adopted by the Swans, surely I'm mature enough to have that box. *My* box.

When I came downstairs for supper, Gordon Swan gestured to me where to sit. It was a gallant sort of gesture, as though I were an honoured guest. I sat opposite him. I was glad there was an easy silence as we ate.

When Hilda Swan rose to bring the pot of tea to the table, Gordon Swan flicked his fingers at me. I looked at him, puzzled. He made signals with his hands and mouthed some words or maybe parts of words.

"Gordon, stop," said Hilda Swan. "The girl doesn't know ASL. She's not deaf! Don't embarrass her."

Hilda Swan turned to me. "His mother was born deaf, Anne. He learned to use American Sign Language. He didn't mean to embarrass you."

I nodded and continued eating. Soon there was an easy silence again, and I could retreat into my thoughts. Images of the day flowed unbidden, a jumble, but always returning to one central moment: the director holding the box and my astonishment at the sudden appearance of the only material link to Mother and Father I'd ever had. Or will have. Why was I given only the photograph of my parents? What else is in the wooden box? Where is the box now?

Ask them right now, Anne. Say: Where is the wooden box?

Words failed me, as they always do, and a gloom swiftly descended and settled on me. I withdrew deep into my refuge.

Instantly, I felt Gordon Swan's attention. I looked at him, and he smiled kindly. He said, "I was reading in the monthly about that Albert Einstein, the fellow who figured out about energy and mass. You study him in school, I suppose, Anne. You know: $E = mc^2$ and that. Well, I was reading that he didn't say a word until he was nine years old, and one day at the supper table with his parents, he said, 'The soup's too hot.' His parents were astonished. 'We didn't know you could speak! Why haven't you said anything before?' Young Einstein answered, 'Well, up till now, everything's been okay.'"

"Oh, Gordon," Hilda Swan said. She laughed and looked at me.

I thought the story was funny, but I was also embarrassed. Of course the director would have told the Swans I did not speak. Would the Swans have seen my medical record? A doctor had examined me when I was four or five years old and had said there wasn't anything obviously wrong with me.

I stood to clear my plate and to help with the dishes. Hilda Swan also rose from the table.

"I'll do those, Anne, while Gordon shows you the garden and barns and henhouse. We hope you'll like looking after the hens and collecting eggs in the morning."

Words came up from the word well to my tongue. My lips formed a *W,* then froze. I stood, lips pursed, holding the shape of a *W. Say it, Anne. Ask: Where. Where. Where is the wooden box?*

Hilda and Gordon Swan watched me in silence, eyes focused on my lips. All of us motionless, like statues.

Hilda Swan broke the spell. "That photograph the director gave you earlier of your mother and father," she said, "was in the box left with you at the orphanage. Your mother was beautiful and your father handsome. You resemble your mother. Both of them, really."

"We'll hold onto the box for a bit, Anne," Gordon Swan said.

I am grateful that Hilda Swan said those things about Mother and Father and me. But the box is mine. They should hand it over immediately.

You agree with me, don't you, Emily?

Gordon Swan showed me the horses, Bonnie and Prince, who adore him, and the cow, Daisy, who adores him, and her new calf, Buttercup, born two days ago and who already adores him. Rex, the border collie, has been staying in the barn and paddock while the calf is so new. Rex sniffed me all over and then looked at Gordon Swan.

"Yes, Rex, she's one of us now," he said, and immediately Rex nuzzled my hand until I scratched him behind the ears. He gave me a paw to shake; then he followed us on the tour of the farm. Gordon Swan showed me the hayloft and how to pitch bales of hay and straw down a hatch into the stable area. Bonnie and Prince can come and go from their stalls into the paddock. He showed me how to open the gate from the paddock to the back field, so the horses and cow and calf can graze all day. He showed me the henhouse and how to change the water in the galvanized watering fountain and how much feed to scatter for the hens, mornings and afternoons.

After I'd had the tour of the farm, Hilda Swan showed me house chores I am to do. Of course, I am a good worker—orphans need to be good at something useful. Being good at drawing and plant identification is not ever likely to earn my keep. How many times did caregivers and matrons drill that into my head?

Hilda Swan saw me eyeing the bookcase in the parlour. "You are welcome to read any of the books, Anne," she said. "And Saturday, when we go to town, we can go to the library and get you a library card. I'm fond of L.M. Montgomery's novels—have you read them?"

The words that came to my tongue were in full-blown gymnastic mode. I wanted to say that I had read every single one of them, twice. And I've read her poetry. And journals. *Say yes, Anne. Just say one little word. She's being so kind. Say something!*

I nodded.

By the time I'd been shown where everything was kept—broom and dust mop, pails and rags, scrub brush and wax—the sun had set. Hilda Swan wished me a good night and hoped I would sleep well.

"Gordon and I are very pleased to have you with us, Anne. We hope you like it here. Tomorrow, we can walk over to the neighbours' place to introduce you and, if you like, you can bring home one of their kittens. They're just now six weeks old."

I didn't need to wrestle with words because Hilda Swan could see the delight in my face, which she echoed with her own delight. "I've been longing for a kitten myself since our old cat died," she said. "Judging from your response, Anne, perhaps we'll need to bring home *two* kittens!"

There was a waning gibbous moon to light my way after the Swans had gone to bed, although daylight lingers late in spring, so the sky was still bright as I found a path across the road that led into the woods, which weren't yet deeply dark. The path led down towards what I knew must be a creek, and I knew that creekside there were likely to be mayflowers.

I was right: there were masses of them. I smelled their sweet fragrance before I saw them.

Mayflowers comfort me. Trailing arbutus. *Epigaea repens.* Earth creeper. I have read it's an ancient plant that has grown here since the last glacial age.

Oh, Emily, there we were again, the two of us, kneeling to pluck a spring offering.

The words the happy say
Are paltry melody —
But those the silent feel
Are beautiful.[2]
The words the silent feel are *beautiful.*

Sometimes.

And sometimes the words I feel are shards of glass cutting my tongue and throat. Or lumps of something I need to spit out and cannot. I swallow the word-lumps whole and suffer as they twist around in my guts.

At dusk by the creek, yes: *The words the silent feel **are** beautiful.*

The way vines of mayflowers cling to the ground reminds me of something I can never quite call to the front of my mind. The woody stems and leathery leaves are so hardy—an evergreen—compared to the pristine delicacy of the flowers. And there's an agreement between mayflowers and fungus, both mayflower and fungus thriving with the help of the other. Like us, Emily. We're symbiotic: you have the words, I have...what do I have?

Sometimes in the spruce needles and leaf litter around mayflowers and other forest flora, I find a perfect beech leaf with ghostly veins that have kept their shape while the leaf has lost almost all substance. Reminding me of me.

In the lingering twilight, kneeling there by the creek, I felt tendrils of possibility and happiness. A room of my own. Good people. Then I remembered the wooden box. It belongs to me. It is the only remaining object that belonged to Mother and Father. The Swans should have given it to me straightaway. Tomorrow, as soon as I am alone in the house, I shall find it.

As I collected a few mayflower vines, I heard a rustling behind me. My heart thudded in my chest.

Rex!

He wagged himself silly and crouched submissively.

Good boy, good dog.

Had I said this aloud?

Sometimes I can't tell, just as when I am reciting your poems, Emily.

Rex accompanied me back to the house, then took himself to the barn. I was able to find a glass, fill it with water, and climb the stairs without waking the Swans. I set the glass of mayflowers on the table by the south window, where earlier I had placed the only book I have ever called my own. There you go, Emily.

The Soul selects her own Society —
Then — shuts the Door —
On her divine Majority —
Present no more — [3]

And then I tried to sleep as I awaited dawn to fetch eggs from the hens and to join the Swans for breakfast. Tomorrow, I would look for an opportunity to search for the wooden box. *My* wooden box. It had been a long day. The first day of my new life.

Day Two: May 16th

They have gone to town this morning! Hilda Swan's sister is ill.

"You'll look after feeding the hens, Anne, and getting your own meals. We'll likely be back by dinner, but you'll be fine here, won't you? Minnie McCreely, our neighbour, the one who has the kittens, will be coming over in a few minutes to help you let the horses and cow and calf into the pasture and help with the hens. She'll stay with you until we return."

I nodded.

The moment they were gone, I began to look for the wooden box that rightfully belongs to me. I searched in all the likely places downstairs. I kept looking out the windows, checking in case Minnie McCreely showed up. It was daunting to invade the Swans' bedroom upstairs. The box was nowhere to be found: not under their bed, nor in their closet, nor on a shelf. I searched the hall closet. Not there. Perhaps they'd put the box—*my box*—in the spare bedroom.

Success! The box was in the bottom of a blanket chest, covered with linens and woolen blankets. My heart was pounding. As I sat staring at the box, I heard a door open downstairs.

"Hello? Anne? It's Minnie, Minnie McCreely, the neighbour. Hilda and Gordon asked me to look in on you. Anne? Are you here? I'll help you with the chores."

I replaced the box—*my box*—in the blanket chest and ran downstairs. I would find an opportunity to fetch it later and take it to my room.

After we had let the horses and cow and calf into the pasture and had collected the eggs and fed the hens, Minnie McCreely and I returned to the house. I ran upstairs, wrote a note, and brought it downstairs to her.

"Are you sure you'll be fine on your own?" she said after reading it.

I nodded.

"Very well, then, Anne. But run over to the house if you need me. Or telephone—my number's there by the phone. Later, you and Hilda can come see the kittens."

In moments, I had the box on my bed in my room. I stared at it. The air around the box seemed to vibrate, the way a patch of evening primrose can radiate an other-worldly yellow, or an Oriental poppy can shimmer such an intense red I could almost faint. The air vibrated as it had when I first looked at the photograph of Mother and Father.

My hands trembled as I opened the box. On top was a letter addressed to me. On the envelope was written: "This letter and the box are to be given to our Anne when she is eighteen years old."

The letter has been steamed open and resealed. By the director? By an earlier director? A caregiver or teacher? This box was at the orphanage all the years I was there. Someone would have opened the letter and read it and

144

then resealed it.

Oh, Emily, imagine: my very own mother and father touched this envelope. This is their handwriting. This wooden box belonged to them.

> *This is my letter to the World*
> *That never wrote to Me —*
> *The simple News that Nature told —*
> *With tender Majesty* [4]

I did not want to rip open the envelope. I ran downstairs to the kitchen, put on the kettle, and carefully held the envelope to the steam. The flap unsealed easily. I sat at the kitchen table and stared at the letter written when I was two and Mother and Father were alive and I was alive and belonged with them. They would have held me and talked with me. Words of love. Words of comfort if I cried. Words of amazement when I first smiled and laughed or first walked or first *spoke*. I was a child then. They were my parents. Arabella Turner Milne and Victor Davenport Milne and me, Anne Arabella Victoria Milne. We three. A complete family.

The kettle whistled and shrieked. I didn't really hear it, but I did smell burning metal when the water ran dry and the base of the kettle began to smoke.

My hands shook so much I feared I would tear the paper.

They were dying, both of them. The pandemic. They had returned to Prince Edward Island, my mother's birthplace. None of my mother's relatives were alive, but a girlhood friend took me in and said she would look after me with her own children until she could find a good home for me.

"Your mother and I know you will be fine, dear Anne," wrote Father. "Remember, nature will always be your friend. You will never be alone. Embrace the wild things of the woods. Perhaps you will continue the botanical work we have done—our notes and drawings are yours now. And keep Emily close, Anne. Memorize poems that make your heart sing and also memorize those that make you weep. You are eighteen now as you read this letter and the journal that your mother and I have kept jointly so you can see what joy you brought into our lives. We have loved you dearer than life itself."

Both had signed the letter, and as I gazed at the loops of their handwriting, I imagined their hands, their arms, their entire bodies. *Oh, Mother. Oh, Father.*

I ran upstairs to look at the rest of the contents of the wooden box.

There was a copy of your poetry, Emily, exactly like the book I'd found at the orphanage. One of the teachers at the orphanage had noticed that I was always reading your poems, and one day she told me the book was mine to keep. "Anyone who loves a book that much deserves to have it," she said.

At the bottom of the box was Father and Mother's

journal. On the first page, *The Flora of Prince Edward Island by Arabella Grace Turner & Victor Davenport Milne.* There are descriptions of plants in both Mother's and Father's handwriting. And sketches and watercolours, so like my own sketches. I leafed quickly through the entire journal. There are notes about weather and birds. And an account of how they met and their marriage. About halfway through, there are entries about me! *Our little Anne was born today. Anne Arabella Victoria Milne.*

"Hello? Anne? Are you upstairs? We're back."

I went to the top of the backstairs and waved at the Swans and held up a finger, hoping they understood I would come downstairs in a minute or two. They smiled. Gordon Swan made an *O* with his thumb and index finger and another hand signal that must mean *Okay*. They went into the kitchen, and I could hear Hilda running water and putting on the kettle. I hope a hole hadn't been burned in the bottom of it.

I am writing the Swans a note saying I have found the wooden box and have read the letter to me from my parents and have found their journal. I will show them the letter. After I've read the journal, perhaps I'll show it to them. Perhaps not.

I'll be forthright with the Swans even if I cannot speak. You will give me strength, Emily, as you always have. The Swans are kind people. I am confident they will not send me back to the orphanage. And already I am confident that I want to stay with them and be adopted by them.

Here on this farm with these gentle people, I will learn to let words come forth rather than be swallowed or choked down. Mother and Father loved me. They loved one another, and they loved me. I have their words. And I have yours, Emily.

In time, I will discover the mystery of why I was taken to the orphanage. Thanks to you, Emily, I have learned to live with mystery and adversity. *The Brain — is wider than the Sky —* [5] And I have learned from flowers—when I look closely at flowers and see how complex their arrangements are, I know my own brain and life are also arranged in such a way.

The wooden box has brought my parents back to me. Oh, Emily, I am no different from my parents: *As Syllable from Sound—* [6] I had a family. Mother and Father and I were a complete family. And we three had another family as wide and deep as nature and poetry. Now I have the Swans, strangers, who chose me to live in this beautiful, quiet place with them and their border collie and horses and cow and calf and hens and fields and woods and creek. Life is unfolding around me. Perhaps now my tongue will be unlocked. And, oh, Emily—I will continue Mother and Father's work. I have been doing this all along, from as early as I can remember. Father and Mother and I are botanists. We three have always had mayflowers. Mayflowers and poetry.

I'll take the note to Hilda and Gordon Swan now. Later, Hilda Swan and I will walk to the neighbours' place, and we will choose a kitten each.

I am happy.

---

1. Dickinson, Emily. *The Complete Poems of Emily Dickinson*. Back Bay Books, 1976. Poem 1161.
2. Ibid, Poem 1750.
3. Ibid, Poem 303.
4. Ibid, Poem 441.
5. Ibid, Poem 126.
6. Ibid.

Deirdre Kessler is a former Poet Laureate of Prince Edward Island and author of over two dozen books for children and adults. Her novel *Darwin's Hornpipe* was published by Penumbra Press in 2023. She worked closely with the creators of the L.M. Montgomery Institute at UPEI; she was project director of the multi-award-winning CD-ROM: *The Bend in the Road: An Invitation to the World and Work of L.M. Montgomery;* and she wrote the epilogue in *L.M. Montgomery and Canadian Culture.* Deirdre is a full-time writer and a sessional professor with the UPEI English Department. Find her online at: DeirdreKessler.com.

SHARI GREEN

Anne of the Silver Trail

Fresh start, last chance, in an unforgiving land.

In memory of Claire Festel, a kindred spirit.

November 1979 – Prince Edward Island

Anne
The Winds of Change

I thought it was over
when Matt lost his job

> they say
> nothing gold
> can stay

but when an offer comes
from a mining camp in the Far
North, Matt asks Maud
her thoughts, and then he asks
me

like my opinion
matters

like I
matter

like maybe—just maybe—they mean
to take me with them.

Maud
Adoption

I said it was practical.

Matt said it was love.

Anne said *where you go*
I will go and it was
decided.

February 1980 – Argent Valley, Yukon

Anne
Beauty

The highway linking Argent Valley
to its neighbouring communities

is mostly paved but narrow, unlined
and without streetlamps
or traffic lights. It's my new
favourite road, simply
because someone was of the miraculous
mindset to name it
The Silver Trail.

A thing has ever so much more
potential
if it bears a beautiful name.

Unexpected

I never expected a land
locked in the frozen embrace
of winter, a land far
from sea and red sand and home
a land from which even the sun
flees for months at a time

a land
such as this

would hold so much scope
for imagination.

Maud
Advice

This land will kill you
if you give it half a chance.

Don't give it any
sort of chance.

Away

Matt's worked nearly every sort of job
there is. Except fishing—grew up on an island
for pity's sake, and he's afraid of the water.
Sometimes I wonder, if we'd stayed

to work his grandparents' farm, would we
have managed to scrape together a living? But
he wasn't cut out for that life. Neither was I
for that matter, and there's no use dwelling

on roads not taken. So here we are, landlocked
again, and Matt's doing work he once did
as a younger man, on our first spell away
from the Island—long before there was Anne.

Anne
Gift

The school bus rumbles across
the bridge, the river
a ribbon of white satin
in the moonlight.

Just beyond the bridge, the driver stops
for Dee and her little sister, Minnie.

Dee plunks down beside me,
same as she's done since my first
day—there aren't many girls
our age, even counting the students
in the next community.

She places a feather
in my hand—pure white, save
for a single dark dot near the tip.

From a snowy owl, she says.

The feather is exquisite
—a simple gift
that tells me

> more than Dee's grin
> or her enthusiastic welcome
> on my arrival

157

more than the way she admires
my has-its-own-mind
long
copper hair

we will be friends
forever.

March 1980

Anne
Aurora

Matt wakes me late
in the evening, beckons
from the doorway, tells me
to bundle up quickly.

A few minutes later, I follow him
outside. The cold slaps
my face, and I'm about
to retreat to the warmth inside
when Matt says, *Look,* and tips
his head back to take in
the night sky. Colour—waves

of green and purple shimmering

across a black canvas dotted
with stars.

I can barely breathe.

Stories

*I've always wanted to study
the ocean,* I tell Dee, *but now
I want to study the sky, too. Understand
the aurora, learn the names
of all the stars, listen
to their stories.*

Dee's eyebrows rise. *Stars
have stories?*

*Everything
has a story.*

My own story tumbles
through my mind. I used to
tell myself it was romantic
somehow, to be orphaned
and unloved, to have nowhere
    and no one
to call home. I imagined

myself a sad heroine
in a grand tragedy
but the truth

was that fear pressed
on my heart constantly—fear
I would misstep once again
and my current foster parents would reject
me. I often left
before they had the chance.

Now, though, I'm part of a story
I want very much to hold on to.

Maud
Saturday Prattle

Linda from next door comes for coffee.
That woman could talk paint off a wall,
all the while pointing out the particular flaws
that made the paint inferior to begin with.

She tells me the entire town believes
Anne is our granddaughter, is shocked
to hear we adopted. *At your age?!* Anne
looks positively faint when Linda launches
into a history of mining disasters. *How*

you can abide Matt working underground
I'll never understand.

I'm not sorry to see her go.

Now Anne's worrying, and I'm in need
of something significantly stronger
than coffee.

Anne
Depths of Despair

I wish Matt had retired
when he got laid off
wish he'd never accepted

a job in the mine, because
I can hardly bear
the thought of him labouring

beneath the surface, darkness
pressing in from every side
headlamp flickering, back

aching, loading the silver-veined ore
that lurks deep in frozen earth, far
from the fragile light

of these winter days, far
from fresh air and hope
should the tunnel

collapse.

Seventeen

Spending hours of this day confined
to school is agony. Geography, our last
class, goes so slowly I can almost feel
the world turning on its axis.

When we're finally free, Dee and I
both get off the bus at her stop.
I need a birthday adventure,
I say. *Let's explore.*

I'm not much for exploring,
Dee says.

After a little convincing
we head out, walk the trail
leading further
into the valley. Layers
of nameless mountains rise
around us.

Isn't it a wonder? I say. *The vast
emptiness. The wildness. The world
is so thin here.*

Dee tugs the zipper of her coat
a little higher under her chin.

Thin? she says.

*The veil between the living
and the dead. Can you feel it?*

Don't talk about death, Dee says.
*Not on your birthday. Talk about
something cheerful—dreams
or friendship.*

We do. We talk
and walk. We don't notice
the clouds rolling in, the first
flakes that build
until they obscure the trail.

Maud
Late

I've been knotted up with worry, yet
here she is, floating into the house, babbling
about mountains and dogsleds.

I'm about ready to toss this cake
in the trash.

Anne
Compunction

When Maud hears we were lost
in the blizzard, rescued
by a trapper who was out on a sled
taking his dogs for a run when
the weather turned, she seems incapable
of deciding whether to throttle me
or burst into tears, and I suppose
I can't blame her.

Matt talks her down, smooths
the tension between us. Even so,
guilt and regret prickle
within me.

June 1980

Anne
Midnight Sun

The days are glorious
and long—light
at all hours. The sun disappears briefly
in the night, but twilight blends into dawn
and the sun returns before we even miss it.

Most of the town has gathered
on the hill above Argent Valley for
a solstice party—a midnight picnic,
a makeshift band, and fireworks
that are festive but less
than spectacular against
the not-quite-dark sky.

When Matt and Maud are ready
to head home, I beg another hour
with Dee and the handful of kids near
our age, then we set off for a party
of our own.

The hour
turns into two.

When I latch the door, tiptoe

across the kitchen, I find Maud
waiting.

Can she blame me for missing
curfew? For staying too long
into a night that doesn't seem like night
at all?

Apparently, yes.
She can.

Downfall

I'm dreadfully sorry
and I tell Maud as much.
Schedules and clocks,
I explain, *are the bane*
of my existence.

She doesn't seem impressed.

It's not the first time
I've not been
where I was meant to be
at the exact time
I was meant to be there, but
is keeping to a schedule
really so necessary? Everyone

seems to think so. Truth
be told, I've had more than one
foster family wash their hands of me
for that very reason.

Maud
Frustration

She is impulsive. Thoughtless. Abandons
good sense and responsibilities the moment
such things become an inconvenience.

Matt is infuriatingly patient. *It's not*
forever.

A noise comes from the hallway, then
a door clicks closed.

I think she was listening, Matt says,
stating the obvious.

I was only speaking the truth, which
she surely knows. Nevertheless, I'd rather
she hadn't heard. I check the hallway
—empty now.

She has a good heart, Matt says.
She'll grow into it just fine.

Anne
The Myth of Forever

Why did I ever let myself believe
adoption was more
than a convenience?

Not forever.

If I'm honest, I've always known
I didn't deserve this home,
this family, this happily
ever after. I've always known
it wouldn't last.

It's not how my story was ever
meant to end.

September 1980

Anne
My Final Year

I've reached the beginning
of the end.

Dee doesn't understand—how
could she? She's always

been wanted. Always belonged
somewhere. She can't imagine
life with her family ending
when she graduates.

As the bus nears the school
on this, the first day of twelfth grade,
I set my mind on a plan.

I'm going to try very hard
to be someone Matt and Maud
will still want to know
once I'm of age, I tell Dee.
I will keep every rule,
meet every curfew,
be as close to perfect
as I can be. Maybe they'll change
their minds about "not
forever."

It's my only hope, and I barely dare
hope it.

Good things end. It's how it is
for people like me. My life
is a perfect graveyard of buried
hopes.

November 22, 9:30 a.m.

Anne
My Solemn Vow

Who knew it was so exhausting
to behave? I won't give up, though
—wake early for my weekend
chores, tell Maud when I'm going to Dee's
to work on our school project, promise
to be home in time for dinner, and silently
vow not to be distracted along
the way by birdsong or frost patterns
or a grand search for snowshoe hares.

Hope is a fragile thing
but each day without catastrophe
it grows.

Maud
Not Yet

Only a fool would attempt
a river crossing before the ice
has been tested and proven safe.

Anne
Seize the Day

I'm anxious to get to Dee's, to share
the revelation that came to me
over breakfast, the revelation
that will almost certainly bump our project
toward the top grade.

My boots squeak on the thin layer
of new snow. I pause near the river bank, marvel
at the immense silence. Glancing toward
the other bank, I spot a line
of footprints—a fox
crossed sometime this morning after
the snow stopped.

It's ever so much quicker
to cross the river
than to walk all the way to the bridge.

Only a fool, Maud said. Only
a fool—or a fox.

Small

I'm hardly bigger
than a fox.

River

In the pale pre-dawn
I step, light
as a fox, onto the frozen
river, hold my breath as if
that will help the river
hold *me*. When the ice

does not give way
beneath my first
tentative steps, I lift
my gaze, wonder
if the fox yipped a song
of triumph
    or relief
when it made the crossing
safely.

A Tale of Wonder

Minnie lets me inside, lingers
in the doorway of Dee's bedroom
while I share the absolute elegance
and wonder of the fox's trail
through pristine snow.

*I had no idea a fox
had such wisdom,* I say.

172

*No idea it could tell
the ice was safe.*

Dee is inadequately impressed
by the fox's wisdom and my
daring, but judging by Minnie's
wide-eyed silence, she's properly
amazed.

November 22, 6:00 p.m.

Anne
Misfortune

Sadly
I was seen
by nosy Linda from next door
who promptly reported my transgression
to Maud.

From Bad to Worse

Matt and Maud, along with Dee's
parents and likely most of the adults
in Argent Valley

are heading to the next town
for tonight's concert—a string
quartet from Whitehorse
performing in the high school gym.

My evening stretches out ahead,
empty. I'm grounded, well and completely,
and I don't dare defy Maud. The words
your last chance still hang in the air.

I must not
leave the house.

I must
do the dishes
and my homework
before they return.

My homework
which I've forgotten
at Dee's.

Juncture

Dee drops off the library book and papers
I need, then leaves. I settle to work, determined
to finish tonight, even if rushing means

I have to sacrifice the top mark. When
the phone interrupts, I ignore it.

It rings again.

I've barely said hello before Dee
breaks in, breathless
—something about
Minnie.

Slow down, I say. *What—*

Missing, she says. *Her coat
and boots are gone. Oh, Anne, I never
should've left her alone—she always begs
to stay home on her own, and she always
regrets it later.*

She tells me she searched everywhere,
is convinced Minnie followed her
to my place.

*But you would've met her
on your way back,* I say.

*The concert's over. My parents
will already be on their way home.
But I can't wait—I have to find her.*

We decide Dee will search
her yard again, check
with any neighbours who
are home, and I
will do the same at my place. Soon
the whole town will be searching
—in a community this size, word
travels faster than icy wind whipping
through the valley.

I bundle up, head out, thoughts
of grounding and punishment
and my last chance swirling
briefly, then vanishing
like smoke. Surely
Maud will understand.

Memory

The beam of my flashlight darts
into corners, behind houses, onto
porches. I bang on doors. The few
people who are home
don boots and parkas, quick
to help.

I picture Minnie lost
in the cold, wonder if Dee
thought to look for footprints
to follow.

A thrill of horror
echoes
in my gut as I remember

Minnie's awe
when she heard about the footprints
of a fox

and a perfect shortcut
for catching up to Dee.

I race
to the river.

Discovery

Midway across the frozen
river, a dark *something*
mars the ice.

Small.
Still.

177

The haunting
howl of a wolf rises
from the valley, piercing
my heart.

Minnie?

In return
a whimper.

Minnie!

Numb

She won't move
      or can't
frozen
by fear after the ice
shifted.

A flash of light from behind me
and several people emerge
from the darkness. Matt
reaches my side just as Minnie
cries out.

I know it looks good and frozen,
Matt says to me, *but the floes
aren't joined solid yet.*

He has no more luck than I do
convincing Minnie to edge
toward shore.

I'll go to her, I say. *I know the ice
will hold me.* And I know I'm the reason
Minnie's in trouble.

Matt won't hear of it.
He moves past me, then he's
on the ice
easing
onto his belly, weight
spread out, creeping
toward the dark
that is Dee's
sister.

Clutch

Others gather
on the far shore, and a spotlight
illuminates the scene.

A voice taut
with fear
rings out—Dee's
mother.

Matt's gentle whispers free
Minnie's mind enough that she's able
to turn back, inch toward her mother
and the pole extended
from the bank.
Finally

she's safe.

My focus returns to Matt, still prone,
peering over his shoulder, then looking
ahead, perhaps deciding the safest
and shortest route.

A hand clutches my shoulder. I glance
around—Maud—and in that instant

she gasps. Matt

scrabbling, broken
through, lower body
submerged. He clings
to ice, struggles
to pull himself from

frigid water, slips
further beneath the surface.

My worst nightmare
rushes, fills, floods
my mind—mine shaft
collapsing, air
vanishing, Matt

gone

but instead of cold earth
it's the river
that swallows him whole.

Beneath

Voices

calling, shouting
screaming Matt's name

muffled, all of it, as if
I am the one
underwater.

Lament

A thousand thoughts
        regrets
—if only

I had listened to Maud
stayed off the ice
been a better example

Minnie would not have landed
in such a predicament

and Matt...

    I can't even think it.

Maud
Eternity

My heart. My Matthew. Please.

November 22, 10:00 p.m.

Anne
The Cost

Maud is with him. I sit
in the tiny waiting
room, insides knotted, clock
ticking louder
than necessary, fluorescent
lights humming, discoloured linoleum,
worn chairs, the smell
of disinfectant.

Two miners trained
in search and rescue pulled
Matt from the river, transported him
to hospital (which is little more
than an outpost clinic in the next town).

The doctor assures us
Matt will be fine, but he must stay
overnight for observation.

He risked himself
for Minnie—and to protect
me. He shouldn't have had to.

Enamoured with the wild beauty
of this land, somehow I ignored
its unforgiving nature, and Matt
nearly paid the price.

I will pay
a different price.

Record-Setting

Has anyone in history ever
blown a last chance quite so
spectacularly?

A Dark Cloud of Woe

When the ones who love
you the most leave you—not
by choice, mind you, but by cruel
fate—it's hard not to believe
every other good thing will also
eventually leave. And so
I always knew tragedy
wasn't finished with me.

I just didn't know I would
bring it upon myself.

I suppose I'm destined
to be without a family
and I suppose

I deserve it.

November 23, 11:00 a.m.

Anne
Truth

Coffee is brewing, and the smell
of it fills the kitchen. Matt and Maud sit
at the table, chatting quietly. They
fall silent when they notice me.

The coffee pot gurgles.

I understand, I say. *And I don't
blame you. Whether they'll take me
back in the system in PEI until
I turn eighteen, or maybe
there's somewhere here—either*

*is fine. But of course
it's not
up to me anyway.*

Maud leans back in her chair, peers
at me with furrowed brow. *For pity's
sake, girl, what are you talking about?*

I dredge the awful words
from deep inside. *I imagine
you're planning to
un-
adopt me.*

Maud's lips twitch.

Not today, she says.

A Wonderful Thing

An enormous silence hovers
briefly, then Maud shakes
her head, says, *That imagination
of yours certainly does
run wild.*

Disbelief
    relief
could it be?

Words spill out, rushed
and tumbling. *Oh, Maud,
I know it. It's as wild
as the aurora in midwinter
and I can't be sorry for that.
It's almost always
a wonderful thing when
imagination runs free. But
do you mean it?
    I can stay
even after this? After
everything?*

I glance at Matt, hoping
for a sign that tells me
this means
what I think it means, but
his eyes are on Maud.

When I look back at her,
she's smiling.

*You're rather dramatic
this morning,* she says.

This moment
seems to warrant it.

Maud
Impossible

Apparently, Anne isn't finished with drama.

The thing is, she says, *I can't promise
to be good. I've been cursed
with curiosity, and I know now
there's no hope of change.*

Exaggeration or not, her words poke
at a spot inside me, and I'm compelled
to right an inadvertent wrong.

I don't want you to change, I tell her.
*If I'm honest, I find you and your imagination
refreshing, and I dare say it's a far sight
better to embrace a curious nature than
to walk through life oblivious to its wonders.*

I feel better for saying it, and it appears
Anne does as well—swooping in
for a hug, which is impossible to avoid.

I know it's only a few more months,
she says into my shoulder, *only*
until I come of age, but
I'm exceptionally grateful.

Anne
Bittersweet

It's always been Matt
who seems to understand me,
but perhaps there's a kindred
spirit in Maud
after all.

I'll be truly sorry
to turn eighteen. Sorry
to come of age and graduate
and see my time with this family
end.

Matt finally speaks up.
Matt, who always knows
my thoughts
    and my worries.

People don't age out
of family, Anne.

March 1981

Anne
Eighteen

If we're lucky in life, we come across
someone who challenges
the lies we tell ourselves, someone
who sits us down and tells us
a different story.

It's hard to believe them, but
if we can let go of the lies for
a moment, let the truth
embrace us, it's a wonder
—an honest-to-God wonder.

Eighteen
isn't the end.
Graduation and even
growing up—not
the end. Believing that
feels like the most beautiful
beginning.

Maud
Frosting

I swear, if that girl isn't home
in time for her birthday cake this year,
I'm never baking another.

Anne
Equinox

After school, Dee finds a length
of green ribbon in her mother's
craft basket, and we head out
along the river, search
for the perfect spot to honour
the sun and the promise
of spring.

We walk a ways, until
the clouds shift and sun
highlights the white bark
of a trembling aspen.

This is it, I say, and Dee
agrees, pulls the ribbon from
her pocket, ties it loosely
around a slender branch.

We give thanks for night
and day, I say, *for darkness*
and light, for winter
and spring, for proof
that endings
are also beginnings.

The ribbon flutters
in the light breeze. Dee
giggles.

She's the perfect balance
to my fondness
for solemnity.

My Whole Heart

There's been talk lately
of closing the mine, debate
about silver prices and the future
of the town. Matt says
time will tell and seems content
to deal with what comes
when it comes. I can't imagine
leaving Dee
now that I've found her, but

this I know:

where Matt and Maud go
I will go
even if
    someday
only
in my heart.

Shari Green is an award-winning author of novels in verse. As a child, Shari fell in love with the original Anne, and is still so enamoured with the story that it features in one of her own books, *Macy McMillan and the Rainbow Goddess*. Shari and her husband spent the first years of their marriage in a mining camp on the Silver Trail and now live on Vancouver Island, BC, on the traditional territory of the Laich-Kwil-Tach peoples. Find her online at www.sharigreen.com (Instagram @shari_green).

MATTHEW DAWKINS

Anne, from nowhere in particular

Another orphan for the road.

My home was a family home, inhabited by relatives that extended well beyond cousins. Auntie Jackie came in and out to "borrow" things we never expected to get back. On Sundays, Uncle Leroy often brought dukunoo and rock cake after church to make sure everyone satisfied their sweet tooth after dinner. The Browns frequently came in through the back verandah, complaining about various small things simply because they wanted to be heard. And everyone had a different name for me.

When I turned ten, I asked my mother to stop calling me *baby girl* because I was big now and she'd been using that name to refer to me since I was born. She smiled at my request in a way I knew meant she had something else in mind.

"Oh, you big now?" she said and from then on, exclusively referred to me as *big girl*. My church friends called me *Rita*—after Bob Marley's backup singer—once I started to sing more frequently at church at our pastor's request. At school, I could not shake *Nunnery*, since I wore a uniform that was a few inches too long. The only person who referred to me by my real name was a man

who was not from our island: the missionary who let me ride in his car. In a way, I preferred his honesty. It made me feel older and especially serious.

He lived close enough to my house that his offer to pick me up on the days track ran late only made sense. My family agreed, and I jumped at the opportunity. I did not know many people in our town who owned a vehicle, and I certainly was not close enough to the ones who did for me to drive with them. That fact somehow made the fabric seats of the missionary's car feel special.

On our way home one evening, the missionary revealed to me that he had never been to our beaches. I told him I didn't go often, either. It was not the rare sight for him that it was for us, but if he'd like, I could take him there. Another excuse, I thought to myself slyly at the time, for another ride. My favourite beach was about an hour away at most, a two-hour journey there and back. But those two hours were worth the view of the Caribbean Sea. If we wanted to get there before nightfall, we'd have to hurry, though. Tomorrow, I had school and he was set for a mission trip into Kingston.

We drove all the way to the coast of the island in his Morris Oxford, right past the sign that instructed us to pay for entry. I assured him no one ever really did unless they were a tourist, but since he was joined by a local, he would be alright. I knew in the eyes of onlookers, he would be assumed to be Jamaican if he were next to me. When we stepped out of his car, I could see peaks of the sea coming into the clearing and pea-sized heads bobbing in and out of the water. I asked that he bring the towel from his trunk so we could maybe watch the sunset. I thought that's what came over my mouth and nose a second later, before I also felt the hand on my throat and a pull yanking me backwards.

I don't remember the last thing I saw before he abducted me, but I vividly remember hearing at once every nickname I was ever given: *Baby girl…big girl… Rita…Nunnery.*

The slow murmur became a babel of voices climaxing: *BABY GIRL…BIG GIRL…RITA…NUNNERY.*

I remember thinking, as my nicknames started to sound like a beating drum, that this would be the last time I would ever hear them. The names I did not take very seriously. The names that represented all the circles of my life were now bidding me farewell.

I came to in this room, with handcuffs on my ankles. I scanned my environment, but it was bare and unfamiliar. No furniture, no people. The wooden beams of the ceiling and the walls were exposed and cobwebbed. Then, hunger forced me to double over as my stomach grumbled. I came to the conclusion that I must have been asleep for a very long time and was now far from home. That idea sent me spiralling. I puked bile. Then the man came.

This man was not the missionary who came to our church and befriended me and my family. The missionary was older and always wore a suit—his appearance was why we accepted his generous donations to buy Christmas gifts for the younger children in the community and trusted his decisions on where we should hold church events. No one had questioned his interest in us, or where the money had come from.

This new stranger had an accent. He was younger and blond, dressed in khakis and a dirty T-shirt adorned with the name of a band I did not know. I realized that the air had a dry quality I was not accustomed to. In the pit of my stomach, I knew I was no longer in Jamaica. Either because he felt sorry for me or simply wanted to hush my sobbing, the man would bring me things if I begged, like extra portions of food and Coca-Cola. When my hair grew, he'd even bring me combs and hair clips. He never spoke, but if I looked into his eyes long enough and begged, his expression would falter and his features would turn sad. But as time went on, that changed. Those small gestures stopped, and when I looked up at him, there was no more sadness, as if it had all run out. In its place, I saw resentment. If I continued to stare, anger.

The man began to leave me alone for hours at a time. At first, I thought it was the opportunity I needed. I'd scream and shout for help, but no one ever came to rescue me. I gave up trying to count the hours he was gone and soon after, the days. He never said where he was going or when he'd be back.

Today, I can't tell what time of day it is. The man stopped switching on the light. He hardly comes to check on me at all, anymore. All that keeps me grounded is a tiny window in the ceiling, so small that most nights when I see the moon, I think it is a light bulb or a beacon.

I've always had a theory: the handcuffs locking my ankles to a metal bar on the floor of the room seem flimsy enough that if I can bend and chew a hair clip just right, I could snap those cuffs right open. I've wasted every hair clip I have on that dream. I've even gone back to reuse the ones I'd given up on. It's taken more tries than I can count, and maybe all my efforts ended up wearing down the lock mechanism or maybe I actually got it right. Either way, today it worked. The handcuffs click open and fall away when I move my legs. The first thing I think to do is try to scream—but nothing comes out. My throat has all dried up. I hold my chest, feel the fast beat inside me, and I try to calm the speed of my heart with more even, deliberate breathing.

I've regained the freedom to run, except looking around, I realize I hadn't thought this far. I've been in the dark for so long, I don't remember in which direction is the door or the light switch. I reach my hands out in front of me, extend them as far as they can go, and then, I walk. I make it to the wall, feel the wooden beams and put two open palms against this new bearing. Using the wall, I keep a steady pace, hoping to end up at the door…when I feel the wall give way. I look harder and I make out that I've made way to a separate room altogether with a tall white object in the middle. Slowly, I step inside.

The closer I get, the clearer the object becomes. It is my height and rectangular. I reach out and feel that the thing is also cold to the touch—metal. My fingers graze its ridges slowly and I reach a handle. This is a cabinet. I pull

open the first drawer and it's full of paper. I pick up a folder resting on the very top. It's easier to make out the black ink against the white paper, and from what I can read, it is an adoption certificate.

I have gone by many names, but on this paper, there is only space for one. Through the dim light, my eyes follow the barely legible pen strokes until about halfway down the page, I realize this name is not one of mine at all. It is a name I hardly even recognize. *A-N-N-E.* I swipe my index finger over the notary seal, confirming that the document is real. I return to the name at the top. *Anne. Who is Anne?*

A car's engine rattles into earshot, and I scramble to refold the paper as I found it. I put everything back into the folder and, before putting it in the drawer, realize there are two, four, six...probably ten files all full of similar certificates. I hear a door open. I shove the folder in the drawer and shut it, dashing back into my own room. I push my manipulated hair clip into my mouth and snap the open end of the handcuffs back around my ankles. A beat after I plop onto my mattress, I hear him.

"I know you're awake." A moment stretches.

My stomach twists. Each slab of wooden flooring creaks under the man's approaching weight. He kicks my mattress. "Look at me." I roll over. I cannot make out many of his features, but I know for sure he is staring. The whites in his eyes do not flinch. "Wipe those tears. We're leaving."

I touch my face to feel a fresh wetness, but I don't

remember crying. I want to ask him, *What about Anne? Who is she? Did you take her from her family just like you did to me?* The man pulls me up by my forearm until my feet recognize that I am standing and what that means.

We stare at each other for a moment, the barely-there light making him clearer at this range. A hovering, seething expression with searching eyes. Under my tongue, I twirl the twisted hair pin that took me countless hours to reshape into a key.

"What? No spiteful words for me today?" he asks.

How does he not see in my eyes that I have discovered the truth? All of those files in his white cabinet must mean that just like he keeps me, he is keeping other girls, I think. But I do not have spiteful words for him. All I want to have is a reckoning for us.

The man releases me when I don't respond to his bait, and exits the room in a huff. The darkness swallows him as he goes to the cabinet and rummages through it. I can hear him open all the drawers and empty them, stacking the folders into a pile on top of the cabinet. The rhythm of the tossing and slamming tells me he doesn't suspect that mere moments ago, I had been there, too.

Stepping backward, I find my mattress and slump down onto it. I imagine our interaction had gone differently. I imagine I twisted out of the man's grip and used the hair pin in my mouth to free myself. In my imagination, I know exactly where to find the front door and I escape through it. When the light meets me, grass, flowers, and trees are being pulled alike by a breeze.

Everything yields. And there are countless homes standing tall on a deserted road that stretches for miles. In this world, I enter every single house without ever needing to knock. None of them are the homes I come from, but I make them into the homes I need. I name them, sleep in them, make dinner in them, and when I'm ready, I take all the supplies that I need from them and start my journey back to my family.

That world only lives in my imagination, though. Until I figure out how to make it real. The man has yet to take me away and I still have the key in my mouth, so maybe there is still a chance I can escape. Maybe I could even get out without him ever being the wiser. I was the fastest girl at my school, after all. I could run quickly once I got into my stride. Before I make up my mind, the whole room suddenly floods with light. Stunned, my eyes snap shut.

As I gently rub them open to a squint, my mattress is first to reintroduce itself to me. It's tinted brown and lying on the floor, riddled with holes and tears. The mould on the wall is a dark green that looks like it smells. There is a staircase ascending to the only door. The man is standing in the middle of the room and lets go of a beaded string connected to a lightbulb and what is truer now stings. I had forgotten it so long ago, I believed I imagined it. There are no other rooms; the filing cabinet is in a tiny closet. The small window I wanted to believe was a beacon is really a hopper. All this time, I have been living in a small basement.

When I rock backwards, the man catches me. "Easy

there. You can't be doing that anymore. You're worth even more money than I expected, little girl." Back home, we shared stories about the people who came before us and what it must have felt like to be sold and bought. I don't ask the man what he means when he mentions selling me, because I think I already know. Once he says it, once we call out the history repeating itself, I'm petrified that my future and my past will be sealed together—shutting me out of my own life.

He undoes the cuffs around my ankles and snaps them onto my wrists, instead. The world turns upside down, and the air is knocked out of me when he tosses me over his shoulder. I want to keep the key in my mouth safe, so I grunt and try to regain my breath through just my nostrils. My weak fists connect with all the parts of him that I can reach, but he is unfazed, hauling me up the staircase and holding together my thrashing feet.

We burst through the basement door and enter the ground floor of the house. There are wooden chairs in front of a light-green mini fridge and in the living room, a bright-red couch against pastel wallpaper. There are many windows, and through all of them, I notice it is raining. I grit my teeth and latch onto a tall chair by the doorway of the living room. It comes with us briefly as the man carries me, before I lose my grip and the chair falls away.

My searching hands then grab a vase. When it slips and shatters, I take hold of a loose fold of wallpaper. As the man and I continue to struggle, we tear the wall open, revealing grey drywall underneath. Then, when the sheet

of wallpaper finally ends, I latch onto the doorknob. I can hear all the rain clearly now, and over his shoulder, I know I am halfway out of the house and halfway in. I try to pull my body out of the man's grip, but it's useless. His hand grabs my wrist and easily yanks my hold off the doorknob.

In seconds, we are soaked. The clear knock of his boots against the wooden front steps turns soft as his feet sink into the muddy soil on the front lawn. And all I see is dirt and rain and the place that has been my prison for so long. For all that time I spent surviving in that house, I don't recognize it from the outside. It doesn't look like any house I've known. It's two storeys, but quiet and empty. As rain pours down, the man opens the door of his van and flings me into it. "Stay here," he says to me. "I'll be right back." He spins briefly, but returns and says what I assume he initially forgot: "Don't try anything."

The man then slams the van door shut and returns to the house. I immediately try to open the door, but it doesn't budge. I lean over to the driver's side. That door doesn't open, either. This van is like the basement, like my locked wrists. Goosebumps prickle the surface of my skin from the cold rain that washed me. Outside, I don't see any other houses except the one I was held in. No people either, just trees and bushes that go up and over endless rolling hills. This feeling is all too familiar. My stomach twists with the most dangerous kind of fear: the kind with a memory. I am in a stranger's vehicle again, at his mercy with no one around to save me. Again, I am about to be stolen away from a home. It is happening all over again. I feel as though I am right back on the seashore in Jamaica. It is a re-enactment, the fear tells me, and there is nothing I can do about it.

The man finally exits the house, holding the binders from the cabinet, and locks the front door. His eyes meet mine through the windshield. My teeth continue to clatter despite my efforts to hold them still. This time, I taste the unmistakable saltwater tears running over my lips. The makeshift key bulges under my tongue, but if I were to free myself now, he would certainly catch me. I would be running alone in the rain, and if I didn't slip, I likely still wouldn't survive the deserted wilds by myself. The man opens the door and steps in, sealing us inside.

Before he puts the key into the ignition, the man clips the seatbelt over me and settles into his own seat without doing the same for himself. The long strap keeps me firmly in place. "You know who you are?" He asks like he is wondering if I remember. I do not pick one of the names the jumbled voices called me that day on the beach. It is not the answer the man is looking for, not really.

He answers his own question. "Nobody cares who you used to be. It doesn't matter. I got your papers and what's on them is the truth. You hear me?" I'm dizzy, then nauseous. I feel hot all over, first in my head, then inside my churning stomach. "Your name is Anne now."

I am Anne. I sink. That adoption certificate is mine. The name I had read earlier—Anne—is the last element

in a long, interlocking chain of lies that has brought me to this place. But unlike the nicknames I was given in Jamaica, this one will change me completely.

Beyond my window, as the house is washed by rain, the kitchen window is illuminated from within. The man must have left a light on. For what feels like miles, I can still see it, even as the rain calms and stars begin to stud the sky. The light is shining out from the kitchen I never knew existed. A part of the big house I never lived in.

Bent, tall grass blurs past us as we drive. The road is deserted except for our car. The heat inside of me is now surging back and forth between my gut and my skull. The man clears his throat. "Listen, we're almost there. When you meet these people, behave right. Pick your head up off the floor and don't bicker. And for God's sake, speak English. Here, in this country, we speak English. These people wanted a boy, so you are already a hard sell. If you mess this up, you won't have the comfort of a mattress or a basement, next time. And if no one decides they want you, you serve no purpose. See those canola fields? Nobody checks them." He gave a cruel chuckle.

I don't know what canola is. I look out my window for it and find bright-yellow fields—the colour of peeled corn. I try to construct a house in the massive garden of yellow—another fantasy—but nothing changes or materializes. My eyes droop. The circulating heat in my body against the cold rain drying on my skin makes me shake. I feel myself falling again.

That's when I see what the man threatens. Through the

rain, my discarded body is in the sea of yellow. I don't move, not at first, but it is as if that version of me senses my eyes on her. She rises, a flowing white gown blowing up around her as we speed by. I whip my head around, but the only thing behind us is dust and the empty road.

"What?" the man asks me. "What is it?"

When I face forward, she is there again. This time, though, she is fully upright and a few metres ahead of us on the dirt shoulder of the road. As we draw near, the headlights travel from her bare feet up to her face, revealing that the woman is not me, but my mother wearing her white church dress. She looks directly at me. The heat blazes up within me again, surging throughout every part of my body as we go past her.

I know when my grandmother pours hot tea from one mug to the next, she is cooling it. It is a tradition we never explain, because it doesn't care to be understood. The heat that surges within me, however, is made to boil. I begin to feel like tradition inverted.

"Why are you making that sound?"

I lurch. In the dead centre of the road, my community now stands. In front of me is my family, as well as all the people who came in and out of my family home. All the people I know. They are clad in the attire they wear to church. Ties, stockings, big hats, suspenders, dresses for all the girls, and button-downs for all the boys. And they wear white. All the people from my life in Jamaica open their mouths, and I hear a chorus of names. My real names.

Baby girl…Big girl…Rita…Nunnery…Baby girl…Big girl…Rita…Nunnery…Baby girl…Big girl…Rita…Nunnery…Baby girl…Big girl…Rita…

The call shakes me.

"What are you on about?"

I no longer see the man. In his place sits the first stranger—the missionary. His face is unchanged from what I can remember, but now I can identify him for what he truly is. The tumultuous cries hammer into me a fantasy that feels like a stone: real. I don't need to be stronger to escape, and better yet, I am not alone. There are named and loved versions of me.

I plunge my head into my palms and spit the key out. I use my right hand, push the hair clip in and twist. The handcuffs open easily.

The man starts talking again, "How—"

I lunge. My teeth sink into his cheek. He lets out an agonizing scream and swerves us off the road. He switches hands and pushes me off. My back collides with the door. We skid along the bank of the road, just dodging where it dips into a grassy ditch that unfurls into more shrubbery.

Free again, I open my mouth and I shout, "You will not take me!" Then, as my heart slams into my throat, I croak, "Yuh haffi kill me first."

I kick, then launch again. And it all goes by quickly. After the first few hits, all I know is I don't want to stop. In that basement, I felt as though I only had my voice and my imagination, but here, I also have my fists, my family, and my future. My voice becomes louder and crystal clear, as I repeat over and over again my version of a battle cry: *"Yuh haffi kill me first!"*

Overwhelmed, the man eventually loses track of which hand is doing the driving. We jolt off the dirt road and plunge where the terrain turns uneven. The van speeds straight for a tree I just barely catch sight of before I'm flung forward.

The crash is so sudden, I'm not sure I hear it at all. I try to catch my breath. There is a ringing in my ears until the rain begins again.

When I reopen my eyes, the van is hugging a tree. Blood is running from a new gash in my forehead and puddles in my eye. Regardless, in seconds, I curl my hands into fists again. Ready, not to fight, but to continue changing my story. But instead of being seated next to me, the man is out of the van entirely, lying on the other side of the glass-studded ditch. The windshield has a hole where he must have been catapulted through. I cough back the smoke and undo my seatbelt, using all my weight and strength to push open the door. Bits of metal are scattered. Smoke masks the scent of gasoline leaking from the car. The man does not look tall while he is horizontal. His right leg has twisted into an unnatural shape.

I spin. There is no one around for miles. Beyond the man and past the ditch is a forest, while the road on the other hand, for as far as I can see, leads nowhere I recognize. Wherever I am, it is not home. I am free, but somehow more alone now than I was to begin with.

Lonelier than I was on that beach and in the basement combined. I buckle, landing on my knees, but the steep terrain is not flat enough to keep me upright, so I go sideways, rolling all the way until I hit the very bottom of the ditch. All the air is knocked out of me. Similarly, mere feet from me, I hear the man take his final breath. In a way, he is taking the van, and the journey, and the way out with him. Maybe if I re-enter the vehicle, I can find the keys. Are the keys even still in there? Will the machine move? I mentally trip over the realization that the key I once hid in my mouth is now also gone.

The sky is turning black, and the rain starts to get heavier. I think maybe I should have waited for another opportunity to strike. I am so angry. I didn't know I could be this angry. And I don't know where to direct it all, or when exactly it became this big. The heat inside of me is still boiling, and I now think I truly understand our tradition. Just like my ancestors, I know what it is to be taken by someone else and to be freed by yourself and that knowledge doesn't shut me out of my own life, but unlocks it.

As I lay on the ground, the blood pumping out of my head merges with the rain and spreads like a fire underneath me. It mixes with the mud and catches my hair. Every strand becomes a dirty, dark red. I wait for the dead man's blood to run downhill and meet me here next, joined, maybe, by the gasoline from the car and mixing in with the rain and the mud to create a pool. I imagine a world where I drown here.

But before the nightmare gets the chance to keep me down, a million hands I recognize reach out for me. At first, I think it is my community—my family coming for me. Then I realize the hands are smaller. Softer. Perhaps they belong to all the other girls like me who've been stolen. Then I realize they're so similar that it almost doesn't matter. In every direction, there is a second hope in the shape of outstretched hands. I am not alone.

Matthew Dawkins is a Jamaican award-winning author and poet whose work explores subject matters including adolescence, race, nationhood, and mental health. *Until We Break* is his debut novel, and his work has also appeared in *Westwind Poetry* and *Pinhole Poetry*, and published with Indolent Books. When he isn't writing, Matthew can often be found daydreaming, speaking to himself, or spending time with the people he loves. Follow him: www.matthewdawkinswrites.com

MERE JOYCE

Where the Dark Goes

They say Green Gallows is haunted...

To the Bear Creek Pit Band,
for my unusual introduction to Anne.

*T*f Mother Nature wept when it rained, tonight she must be in a rage.

Mud splashed off my sneakers as we headed down the laneway, the thunder cracking against the sky and prompting me to pick up speed. Over an hour trudging through a drizzle that had steadily increased to a full-on tempest made me certain I would never want to live in the sea. The mermaids and water nymphs could keep their shining waters. I wanted only to be dry.

"Is that the place?" Davy started to run ahead, but I grabbed the back of his shirt to keep him close.

"Hey, remember when I promised to keep you safe?" I asked, as he shot me an annoyed glance over his shoulder. "That means I make sure the house is safe, too, before you go bulldozing inside."

Davy looked like he was going to argue, until his eyes flickered over my cheek. "Okay." He turned away with a meek nod.

My cheek throbbed as I touched it with the back of my hand, and I gently urged Dora to move a little faster, reminding myself that the hours in the rain—along with a full day riding buses and taking the ferry from one prov-

ince to another—were worth it. Blewett may have gotten a hit on me, but he hadn't reached his intended target. Davy and Dora were exhausted and drenched, but they were otherwise unharmed. The twins were free. And now, the house we'd been travelling to was right where Rosalia had said it would be. Beyond the woods, past the hollow, down the laneway. A place where we would be safe.

Provided we could actually get inside.

"It's so big," Dora whispered as we neared the porch.

She was right. The house seemed taller than it should be, and the shadows it cast made it feel positively massive in width. I was used to small quarters, places so cramped you could never properly stretch your neck, never mind your imagination. But here, the very house seemed to stretch, spreading as if it might someday merge with the night.

The three of us approached the door slowly, and I held my breath as I glanced through the dark windows along the side of the house. More thunder rumbled overhead, and the wind pushed against my back, urging me on. My hand trembled as I twisted the doorknob, until the click of the latch tickled through my fingers like a handshake— almost as if the house itself were welcoming me inside.

Perhaps it was a little disrespectful to Mother Nature and her woes. But as the door swung open to reveal the dark corridor within, my swollen face broke into a smile.

"Thank you, Rosalia," I whispered into the dark. "And your obsession with old, abandoned places."

I ushered the twins across the threshold before closing

the door behind us. The rain hammered furiously against the windows, trying to join us inside, but the glass kept the storm at bay as we slipped off our muddy shoes and placed them on a cobweb-riddled mat. According to Rosalia, this house had been abandoned for three decades. But despite being unlocked for anyone to wander in, it was still fully intact, furniture and all.

"You don't want to go to a creepy place like that," Rosalia said when I spoke to her yesterday. I could still hear the payphone crackling as she tried to convince me not to run away with the twins, and tried to warn me how hard life was when you had to pay your own way in the world. "Green Gallows is what they call it, you know. The twins won't be any better off there than with Blewett."

The floor groaned under my bare feet as the three of us stepped further into the house, my hands wrapped around their little fingers as my face throbbed with a truth Rosalia didn't understand. There was no way this house was more dangerous than Blewett. Rosalia might call this undisturbed place unnerving. But to me, Green Gallows was a haven.

The twins and I stopped at the foot of the stairs, the beautiful oak banister curving out of sight as it rose to the upper floor. Blackness swallowed all but a couple of the steps, another thing my former foster sister would probably consider foreboding. But where she saw places for demonic things to lurk, I saw nooks and crannies that would hide me from the monsters that lived outside of these walls.

"It's quiet in here," Dora whispered as I pondered what secrets the darkness held. But her words were followed by a soft creak above us, and for a moment, my spine stiffened. The whole house then groaned as the wind howled outside and a boom of thunder shook the door behind us, a sharp reminder of why we were lucky to finally be inside.

"Let's check out the rooms," I said. "Then we'll find somewhere to put our things. Okay?"

We made a sweep of the house's main floor, wandering through a formal sitting room, a large country kitchen, and a small den. The rooms were dank and dirty, but there was a charming quality to them that lifted my tired spirits. Despite Rosalia's misgivings, the house didn't feel like an ominous destination. I could imagine a world of cherished memories preserved beneath the filth.

We were secure here. We were safe. And we were finally someplace dry. Now, I just had to get us dry, too.

The upper floor of the house contained three bedrooms, along with a linen closet and a small bath. The hallway reeked of mildew, but as we ventured into each room, I was delighted to realize that not only were the beds still in place, but the sheets were, too.

"Who would want to sleep on musty old sheets?" Davy pulled a face.

"You will, when you realize how chilly it gets with no heater in the house," I told him.

Davy gave up arguing and instead ran ahead to look for spiderwebs, while Dora stayed by my side, silent as she

took in the strange wonder of an abandoned, furnished house. In one room, we even found an oval brooch decorated with a border of amethyst, sitting untouched on top of an old-fashioned dresser. To think no intruder had pocketed the jewellery was nothing short of a miracle.

I was curious to know who was to thank for such grace.

The last bedroom was mostly empty, a spare with nothing in it aside from a chair, a chamber pot, and an old bed. Satisfied that the house truly was abandoned, I dropped my bag on the duvet and dug out our pajamas. It would be strange wearing nothing but my hand-me-down nightgown in this odd, old house. But Green Gallows was located in the middle of nowhere, and the very thought of staying in my cold, wet clothes all night sent a shiver down my spine. I took the twins' clothes to the bathroom, where I discarded my own sodden things and let the worn-thin cotton of my nightgown settle comfortably over my skin. Then I hung the dripping garments over the edge of the grimy tub before returning to the spare room.

"You should get some sleep," I said to the twins once I had returned. They'd been on the run all day, and musty or not, the sheets would keep them warm while they rested.

"I can't sleep here," Dora said. She sounded exhausted, but her fretful eyes were wide in her tiny face.

I stroked her hair, wondering how I could put her more at ease. "How about I tell you a story?"

Davy was quick to roll his eyes. "Your stories don't have enough blood and guts in them," he whined.

I rolled my own eyes back at him. "I don't think gore is what we really need on a night like this." I looked at them, tapping my lips in thought. "But you know what? In the den downstairs, I think I saw some bookshelves. Maybe there's a book or two I could bring up to read."

Davy opened his mouth to argue, but his eyes once again caught the shadows of my bruise, and he soon dropped his gaze. His guilty frown wrenched my heart. I wasn't sorry to have this injury when it meant Davy's skin remained untouched. I was only sorry he had to see how it happened.

"I'll stay with Dora," the little boy said in a more subdued voice. "You can get a book for us to read."

I didn't like the idea of leaving the twins alone, but the spare room was safer, especially if I left them with the flashlight. They had been through enough. They didn't need to be creeping through the dark in their bare feet. I dug the flashlight out of my bag and handed it to Dora, hoping the batteries still held a decent charge.

"I'll be quick," I told her. "We'll use the light to read when I'm back." I turned to hold Davy's shoulders, leaning in close so he could see my eyes in the darkness. "Stay here. And *don't frighten her.*"

Davy swallowed and gave me a solemn nod. I nodded, too, then pulled both twins into a fierce hug before heading back to the main floor.

I took my time as I moved through the house, treading carefully to keep from tripping while I admired the home's eerie décor. In the kitchen, I paused to draw a

heart in the dust on the big, sturdy oak table, tracing an *A* in its middle and wondering why no one had ever claimed Green Gallows for themselves. For a moment, I wished I could be the one to call this place home. Yet even in my fantasies, I knew this was no place for the twins. It was better than Blewett's house. But it would never be where Dora and Davy belonged.

"Come on," I told myself sternly. "Stop dawdling. Let's find a good story and go back upstairs."

I opened the door to the den, then quickly found that my plan was not to be. There were no books. Empty shelves lined one wall, and an empty writing desk sat next to the door. There was nothing else in the room except for a well-worn chair, positioned at a curious angle and tucked into the shadows of the back wall.

I followed its direction to see it facing the room's only window.

"Must be something pleasant out there," I mused as I noticed the drawn shade. "Why else would you leave all the shelves empty, yet still put your best chair in a room like this?"

The floor above me creaked in response to my words, and cold snaked between my shoulder blades as I raised my eyes to the ceiling. Davy was likely pacing the spare room above the den, his short legs forever unable to stay in one place for long. I opened my mouth to admonish him, but before I could yell out a warning, the creaking came to a stop.

When silence returned, I let out a slow breath, my

shoulders sagging in relief.

And then the window shade rolled up.

SNAP!

I jolted as the shade rattled up to the top of the frame. Lightning flashed against the dark glass, and for a moment I was shocked by the temporary illumination of my own reflection. My orange braids combined with the old white nightgown made me look like a candlestick set aflame, strangely fitting in this gloomy old house. I turned so my bruised cheek was not visible, and for a fleeting instant I smiled, imagining how lovely it would be to be a bright candle in a quiet sanctuary like this.

When the lightning's glow faded, so too did my own vanity. Instead, I found myself drawn to a duller, grey shape in the glass—the shape of something else reflected in the room behind me.

The shape of a man, as still as a picture, sitting in the chair to my back.

"I-I'm sorry," I stuttered, my heart suddenly in my throat. I could barely make out two legs clad in trousers, and a large, withered hand resting on one thigh. But the features of his face were lost to the shadows. "I didn't mean to disturb you. I thought this place was abandoned. I just came in from the storm so the twins could get dry. Please…I didn't think anyone was here."

The man in the reflection made no reply to my apologies. His silence was unnerving, and with a flare of panic, I forced myself to turn. The edges of my nightgown swayed in a dramatic flourish as I spun, but when I faced

away from the window, the chair was empty.

With a cautious step back, I scanned the room, wondering if I was making men out of shadows, or if the shadows were only doing their best to conceal the man. My eyes caught on the open doorway, and as my heart pounded unsteadily, I remembered the twins upstairs, alone. I started to move forward, until a sweep of cool air rustled against my back. My shoulders tensed again, my step freezing as goosebumps prickled over my skin. A soft rasp of icy breath creeped across my neck, and cold fingers stabbed at the base of my skull. I gasped, the cold running under my hairline—under my very skin—until it pierced the soft folds of my brain.

The dark den dropped away as the world around me swayed, unfocused and foggy. Then, slowly, the fog gathered, shaping itself into a vision that floated in my mind's eye.

An old man in this very room. A dead man, laid out in his coffin, his whole body covered with flowers. A little piece of his garden, keeping him company in death.

Slowly, the iciness retreated, and I sagged forward, tears trickling from my eyes.

"A garden," I whispered in surprise. "That's what's beyond the window. You're a ghost. And outside this den is your garden." I wiped a hand against my face, ignoring the burn of my cheek as I wiped away my tears. "This *was* your garden, at least. Can someone have a garden, even if they're dead?" The idea blossomed in my mind, and with it came the strange sensation of soft warmth, as if I were

suddenly standing in a field of sun-drenched petals. "What a lovely end that would be," I mused. "To go on working in your garden forever."

The rasp of breath sounded again, this time in front of me, and when I blinked, the man was once more sitting in his chair. My eyes had adjusted to the darkness by now. But still the man was only half present, tucked into the depths of the shadows like a trick of my tear-blurred eye. I peered harder at him, trying to work out the truth of his shape. He remained an illusion, and if I tried to get any closer, I was sure he would altogether disappear.

"I hope you don't mind if we stay here," I said, trusting the vision he'd shared was meant as an offer of peace. "For a little while. I had to get the twins out, you see. I made a promise to keep them safe. But we don't have anywhere else to go…and you have such a lovely home. Even with the cobwebs, and the creaks. Even those are lovely, in their own way."

The floor above us groaned again, and my voice trailed off as I listened to something roll and stretch with a horrendous whine. It moved from one side of the house to the other, and my eyes trailed along the ceiling until, all at once, the sound gave way to a series of enormous thuds.

Dora screamed, and Davy howled my name.

"Anne!"

I bolted for the door, forgetting all about the old man as I dashed back through the kitchen. The noise overhead bounced and echoed down the stairs, bellowing like an

enormous, hollow drum. I pictured the twins, their little bodies tumbling down the steps, and with a cry of horror, I reached the doorway leading back to the sitting room.

My hand grabbed the doorknob at the same moment the thudding whine stopped. I paused, my heart in my throat as I stared at the sliver of black hallway beyond the opened door.

And waited.

WHAM!

Something crashed to the foot of the stairs.

I raced forward to see what it was. My bag had been tossed down the stairs, clothing and food strewn across the entryway. I left the mess and turned for the stairs instead.

"Dora?" I called as I continued to run, my nightgown hitched above my knees so I didn't trip. "Davy?"

"We're here, Anne!" Davy called. He was standing in the hallway, Dora clutching one hand and something small clutched in his other.

"What happened?" I asked, breathless as I reached the hall. "Are you okay?"

"We're fine," Davy said. He looked guilty again, and his free hand disappeared behind his back as he spoke. "We were just exploring."

My cheeks flushed, fear making my temper flare. "I told you to stay in the room!"

Dora stared at the ground, while Davy appealed to me with eyes so sweet and doe-like they made me want to weep.

226

"I'm sorry," he said. "Dora said she wanted to wait for you in the hall. And then I saw…"

He stopped talking, as I held out my hand.

"What did you take?" I asked.

With a sheepish grin, Davy held out the amethyst brooch I'd seen in one of the other bedrooms. I recoiled at the sight of it, and my temper threatened to flare again.

"You shouldn't have touched that, Davy!" I said in a low voice. "It's not yours."

"I was only looking, I swear!" Davy pleaded. "But as soon as I grabbed it, these horrible noises started. And then something crashed!"

"It was our bag that crashed," I said. Which meant that someone else had been in our room. I didn't think it was the man in the den, though. He'd been with me when the noises began.

I studied the brooch Davy had taken. The purple stones caught what little light came from Dora's flashlight, and they partook in their own despondent dance as I carried the brooch back into the bedroom. My eyes swept across the room's mauve curtains and its sturdy old four-poster bed. Then I crossed to the dresser, clearing away the dust and placing the amethyst brooch back where it had been.

As soon as I released the brooch, a barbed wire of ice wound around my hand.

Pressure squeezed my fingers, and I cried out in pain. The touch was a clear cold warning that the room's resident was not happy we had taken the brooch. But as

the frozen grasp met mine, it happened again. Like downstairs, my head grew foggy, until the discomfort formed itself into another vision. This time it was of a woman, stern and proud—and blind. The man I had seen after his death. When the vision showed me the woman, she was still alive.

She walked through the hallway until she reached the stairs. She misstepped, scrambled for the banister, failed to find support. Tumbling, she rolled, over and over until she landed, twisted and broken, her blind eyes forever wide with fright.

The ice against my hand cracked open, and I pulled my arm to my side, horrified by the image of the woman's lonely death.

"I'm sorry," I whispered, stepping back from the dresser. The woman's death was tragic, but that did not mean her warning held any less weight. The man wasn't the only one in the house. This other ghost had no intention of letting us lounge about, pretending we belonged here. "We didn't mean to intrude. And we won't stay, if you want us gone. But I...I need to keep them safe. Please, just let us stay until the rain stops. A little time for the storm to pass, and then we'll go."

I felt a cold pressure touch the bruise on my cheek, and I gripped the edges of my nightgown, shivering as I waited for the ghost to appear. But she did not. Instead, the pressure against my cheek lightened, and the room became warmer. With a nod of gratitude, I turned away from the dresser and walked back out into the hall. I grabbed one twin in each hand and firmly pulled them to the spare room. Our things could wait until the morning. For now, I wanted to get a door between them and the ghost before the woman changed her mind.

"Anne?" Davy asked with a timid breath as I helped them crawl under the covers. "What was in that room with you?"

I tucked them in and smoothed the sheets before I answered. "Once, a long time ago, you asked me if I knew where the dark goes during the day. Do you remember that?" I gave him a steady look as I swept a fringe of hair from his eyes. Davy shook his head. "Well, I told you it went around the earth. Which is true. But…it's only part of the truth. The other part is that some kinds of dark don't go anywhere. Some of them only hide. Where it's safe. The thing in that room…she understands that all I want is for you two to be safe as well."

"I want to go home," Dora said.

"That place wasn't home," Davy muttered.

Dora looked at her brother, then turned to look at me. "I know," she said after a moment. "But I'd like to go home, all the same. Wherever that is."

I tried to smile, but my lips could barely budge, so I kissed the top of her head instead. "You'll have a wonderful home someday, Dora. Both of you will."

The twins nestled into the bed, and I sat on the floor next to them, my chin on my knees while I watched the door. Nothing creaked or rolled outside of the room. Only the wind, the rain, and the twins' restless squirming

kept me company, until, bit by bit, exhaustion caught up with us. Davy fell asleep first, then Dora a few moments later. When my own head began to droop, I lay down on the floor, tucking one arm under my head and curling into a ball, my eyes still trained on the door.

I did not intend to do anything more than doze. But the sound of the twins' gentle breathing and Mother Nature's fiercer tears was a lullaby of its own.

Soon, the peculiar, haunted peace of Green Gallows rocked me to sleep.

My dreams were full of thunder, the distant rumbling growing closer and more insistent until it was so loud I bolted upright on the floor. My heart pounded in time with the thudding, a persistent rhythm that rose up from beneath me like someone shoving a broom against the ceiling on the floor below. I held my hands to my chest, trying to decide if the woman had changed her mind about letting us stay, after all. But as the thudding continued, I realized it was not coming from the woman at all. The spare room was directly above the den. It was the old man trying to get my attention.

"What is it?" I whispered into the night.

My answer was a flash of lightning so bright it made me wince. I stood, the soles of my feet pressing against the cold floor as I waited for the flash to pass. But the light continued to shine, and after a few confused seconds, I crossed to the window—only to discover it wasn't lightning at all.

Stunned, I watched as a truck sped through the mud,

its headlights beaming as it roared down the laneway before squealing to a stop near the house. My heart skipped a beat as I silently implored the vehicle to kick into reverse and head back the way it had come. But all too quickly, the truck's engine cut, and the driver's door opened wide.

A familiar man climbed out of the truck.

"Blewett!" I gasped.

My foster father clicked on a flashlight, sweeping the smaller beam over the house's windows as I jumped back from the window. How could he be here? How could he *know?* I paid cash for our tickets. I wore my hood up to keep my bright hair and bruised cheek hidden. I didn't tell anyone where we were going.

Anyone. Except for Rosalia.

"She wouldn't tell," I said to myself as I retreated further into the room. "She wouldn't…"

I stopped, pained with the agony of betrayal. Rosalia made it clear she didn't want me taking the twins away. She didn't think I could support them because she knew all too well how hard life was without any money. She thought the twins were better off with someone like Blewett, if it meant they had a place to sleep and food in their bellies.

"Anne!"

Blewett banged on the front door, and I screamed before I could help it, knowing that the door wasn't locked.

"What's wrong, Anne?" Davy asked in a sleepy voice,

roused by my alarm.

Before I could speak, Blewett pounded the door a second time. Dora startled awake with a cry, and Davy sat upright, eyes wide as he hugged his sister. I frantically looked for a place to hide as I heard the door click open below me.

"We need to get out of this room!" I said. I pulled the twins out of the bed, tucking them under my arms as I left the spare room and hurried them into the woman's bedroom instead. "Hide under the bed!" I hissed.

"Anne!" Blewett raged from inside the house. His feet stomped through the entryway, pausing only a moment before he started up the stairs.

I ran into the hallway and closed the door behind me, waiting until Blewett caught sight of me before I fled back to the spare room. I ran for the window, pushing at the lock and banging my fists against the latch until it finally gave. Shoving up the pane, I wasted no time in climbing over the sill. The roof was slick under my bare feet, and it took three tries to balance enough to let go of the wooden ledge. When I did, I shimmied along the shingles, wiping rain from my face with one hand as I turned back to close the window behind me.

The glass was halfway down when the spare room door burst open. Across the small distance, Blewett's cold eyes met mine.

"You little brat!" he screamed.

I gave the window one last shove, ignoring his insult as I crawled as fast as I could over the east gable of the

house. Blewett struggled with the window, cursing and banging his fists until he finally got it open. He stuck his head outside to figure out where I'd gone, and the fright of seeing him so close made me slip. My legs splayed out across the roof, and I grabbed hold of a vent pipe, curling my fingers around the cold metal as I scrambled to get traction with my feet.

"Get back here, Anne!" Blewett roared.

My soles scraped against the shingles, although their rough texture gave me a stinging semblance of footing. Carefully letting go of the vent pipe, I continued to the south side of the house, rounding the corner of the roof as I searched for the room with the amethyst brooch. Arms and legs shaking, I clawed at the shingles, straining my muscles to reach the window before my strength gave out. When I got to the wooden sill, I wedged my foot against a peeling shingle and pushed up until the window cracked open. My heart skipped a hopeful beat, and I pushed harder, bracing my legs and watching for the moment I could dive inside.

The glass inched slowly upwards...then suddenly bolted up. I fell against the ledge, hands gripping loosely to the sill as I looked up—to see Blewett standing inside the room, Dora and Davy in his muscular hands.

Blewett's eyes were narrowed slits of anger, and he moved at an unhinged speed, one arm wrapped around the squirming twins while his free arm shot out to grab hold of me. I braced for the impact of being dragged through the window. Instead, I felt only a massive tremor

shuddering through Blewett's fist where it was tangled in the fabric of my nightgown. I saw the twins pull away from him as he toppled forward, his eyes widening with something I'd never seen before—fear. I watched the strange way he trembled, then shifted my gaze to where two slender hands pressed against his back. My stare met the ghostly white spots of the woman's sightless eyes as she forced him farther away from the twins.

Blewett crashed forward, trying to use me to block his path as he fell. I grabbed the edge of the window, twisting out of his hold as Blewett fell over the sill. His large body flailed, his fingers curling over the window's ledge, and with a cursing howl, he swung himself forward to reach into the room. Another scream soon echoed from inside—from Davy—as Blewett grabbed the little boy's arm and pulled him over the windowsill. Dora screamed, and she tried to hold onto her brother's waist to keep him from going over the edge.

"No," I whispered aloud, a promise to myself and the twins both. My foot came out of its wedge, and I lunged across the window. "NO!"

My hands descended over Blewett's, and my nails gouged his skin as I pried at his fingers. Blewett's hold on the windowsill gave, and he growled in pain as he tried to swat me away. I caught his wrist, wrenching it back at the same moment I peeled his hand off Davy. The twins fell into the waiting cradle of the ghost's cold arms, and for a happy instant, my whole body hummed with relief.

Then the hum flared into a wild spark of agony as

Blewett grabbed hold of my braids to drag me down the roof with him. We fell together, under the rumbling boom of Mother Nature's wail.

I awoke to gentle pushing and prodding. But when my eyes fluttered open, I was alone, tucked under the soft sheets of the spare bed. The room was dim, but bright, like the whole world was lit by a soft, hazy sun. I lay under the covers, sleepy and content, until hints of red and blue tinted the light. Then I slowly sat up, the edges of my ears tingling with the muted sound of sirens.

The room was bright, but when I climbed out of the bed, I could see the rain still falling outside the window. I saw an ambulance parked in front of the house, and a crowd of strangers huddled together under black umbrellas, watching the paramedics work. I wondered where these people had come from and who had alerted them to trouble. A ribbon of searing pain shot across my scalp as I searched their unknown faces, until my curiosity gave way to a different sort of pain as my gaze alighted on the twins.

Dora stood holding the hand of a middle-aged woman. Davy stood next to her, holding the hand of a girl closer to my age who I guessed must have been the woman's daughter. The twins were crying, and the sight of their tears filled me with such intense grief that the ground beneath me became unsteady. I swayed, lightheaded, until Davy looked up at the window.

He stopped crying and his eyes widened, but then I saw him grin, and with frantic, almost wild enthusiasm, he waved. The girl beside him brushed a hand along her dark bangs, her gaze sweeping up to see what he was waving at. She looked far more startled than Davy to see me, and I staggered to the side as a stretcher—two stretchers—rolled past the crowd. The girl followed the second stretcher with her eyes. Her stare caught on the red braid dangling from its side before she looked back up at me.

We both seemed to understand together.

Another wave of pain engulfed me, and I struggled to keep my balance, struggled not to follow the rolling sensation into the clanging dark of the ambulance. I pressed my feet into the ground and placed my hands against the cool glass of the window to keep me steady.

"Please," I said as the lingering sensation of the stretcher faded. "Take care of them."

For a moment, the girl continued to watch me. Then her brow furrowed, and she looked at the two children. Her arm snaked around Davy's shoulders, drawing him tight against her side as she returned my stare. I could see the fierceness in her expression, along with the doting way the older woman gazed at Dora. I suddenly felt calm as I remembered what happened here last night. The ghosts would not have allowed Davy and Dora outside if they thought there was more danger there. Whoever this dark-haired girl was, I somehow knew that she and her mother would care for the twins now that I was gone.

The thought of being separated from Davy and Dora was too much, though, and I ran out into the hall, bounding down the stairs to the front door. I wanted to follow them, wanted to stay by their sides forever, in whatever way I could. But the world outside was dreary next to the comfortable calm of the house, and as I reached for the door handle, the wet dimness outside made me remember the last piece of the night's puzzle— the last person who played a part in the tragedy so recently occurred.

Whatever had happened to Blewett, he was no longer here. He was gone, and he would never hurt anyone again.

But I knew there would be others like him. And there would be others like me, who needed to get away. Who needed somewhere safe.

A familiar rasping noise sounded to my back, and my hand pressed against the window next to the door, finger trailing a heart in the dust and tracing another *A* inside of it before I turned.

The ghosts were standing on the stairs. Except they weren't ghosts. I could see them clearly, the old man next to the banister, and the blind woman, tall and proud, two steps up. They looked similar, like a brother and sister who were close in life…and in death.

The old man smiled at me, while the blind woman held out her hand, beckoning me to join them. Welcoming me to stay.

"You helped me keep them safe," I said. I looked out

the window at the flashing lights, at the strangers crowding around to watch the ambulance drive away. A soft smile spread along the cheek that no longer hurt as I pressed my fingers to the heart in the glass one final time. Then I crossed the hall to join the siblings who had warned me of Blewett's arrival. Who had done their best to keep him away from the twins. "Can I do the same?" I asked as I stopped by the banister. "Could I keep this place for the others like me—for anyone who doesn't have anywhere else to go?"

The ghosts didn't answer, but they didn't have to. The whole house brightened more, and the scent of freshly blooming wildflowers filled the air as I took their hands in my own. This house had stood empty for decades, and I would do my best to make sure it stayed standing for decades more. Not as a gallows warding off trespassers. But as a haven, for all those who followed where the dark goes in the hopes of finding somewhere a little more like home.

Mere Joyce was first introduced to Anne Shirley while playing clarinet for her high school's production of *Anne of Green Gables: The Musical.* After swapping music for stories, Mere went on to become an author of more than ten books for middle grade, young adult, and new adult audiences. Her writing includes contemporary tales, fairytale fantasies, high-action mysteries, and her personal favourite–ghost stories. When she's not writing, Mere can be found teaching library studies or spending time at home with her family in Nova Scotia. You can find her online at merejoyce.com, or on Instagram @merejoyce.

SUSAN WHITE

Matthew Insists on Ripped Jeans

Who's the trendsetter now?

To Emma

*A*nne picked up the dusty volume off the table. Since coming to live with the Crawfords a month ago, she'd walked by this table and seen the faded blue book every time she came upstairs. She had just never picked it up until now. The jolt of emotion seeing the title of the book had been too powerful and frightening, and she'd always hurried by the table, turning her gaze away quickly. Anne already knew this book. She'd taken the illustrated volume everywhere after receiving it on her sixth birthday and had read it so many times that she'd almost memorized parts of it. Reading it out loud became a bedtime routine with whichever parent tucked her in. But those days were long behind her.

"Are you a reader?" Rosemary had asked Anne the day she first arrived. "We've got lots of books around. My brother doesn't read much, but I've always liked a good story. That book on the table was my mother's when she was a girl. She placed it there years ago, so it doesn't seem right to move it…but you can read it if you want to. I've never read it, but I know movies and TV shows have been made of it over the years."

The third foster home had no books at all, but the

social worker, Sandy Dixon, had dragged Anne to the library at least once a week. At first, Anne came home with an armful of books but never opened them, until the week she'd picked five books from the *M* section. Anne had read all five books in two days, but trips to the library stopped when Mrs. Dixon found out what she'd done with them.

"Whatever possessed you to burn those library books in the fire pit, Anne? I thought you'd love them, each one having your name in the title. It's fine if you didn't like the books, but why would you burn them?"

Anne had shrugged her shoulders and walked away, unwilling to show this woman any of the emotion reading those five books had stirred up. But that was in the past. Standing in the hall, looking down at the faded old blue cover of the familiar book, she almost took the same approach. Instead, she picked it up and took it into her room.

Anne sat down on the edge of her bed, remembering the cover of the library book edition. Somehow she'd forgotten about her own copy until she pulled the book off the shelf at the library that day. How had she forgotten a book she loved so much, a book her mother had also loved before her, even choosing to name her daughter Anne-with-an-e? Anne flipped through the pages and closed the old book, recalling the last time she'd held her own treasured copy. A crash. Metal crunching, glass shattering. Chaos and confusion, sadness and misery. How could she possibly read this book again? Maybe

instead of reading *Anne of Green Gables* this time, she'd try to become the main character and pretend she was living Anne Shirley's life rather than her own.

"Rosemary will be Marilla, and Clayton will be Matthew," Anne slowly whispered to herself. "And that old woman who was here when I got dropped off can be Rachel Lynde. I'll be imaginative, chatty, and cooperative—not like the troubled foster children in the book who threaten to burn people's houses down or put poison in their wells."

Two weeks later, Rosemary stood at the stove, stirring a pot of chili. Anne's behaviour was getting stranger every day, but Violet assured her that it was probably just the girl's way of readjusting to a new home environment. Anne's new social worker, Trudy Allan, would be coming by for her regular visit in a few days. It made sense that foster kids had trouble adjusting to new things and different surroundings. Rosemary tasted the chili and added a dash of cayenne. Besides, what did she and Clayton know about raising a teenage girl? Anne had asked her if they'd wanted a boy, and strangely, that had been Rosemary's original pitch to her brother when she'd first brought up the idea of taking in a foster child. She'd suggested they foster a boy who could help out with the chores. Hearing about all the drama Violet's granddaughters often caused also made Rosemary leery of taking in a teenage girl.

"These aren't the olden days, Rosie. You can't get free labour out of some poor orphan just by giving them a roof over their head and three meals a day." Clayton had given her one of those incredulous looks of his.

"You're right. Just forget I said anything. It was a bad idea—we are completely unprepared for a foster child." Rosemary returned to the dishes she was washing.

But instead of forgetting about it, Rosemary had made a call to inquire about fostering. She'd been told about the immediate need to place a thirteen-year-old girl who, if a home could be found in this area, would be able to continue attending the same school she'd been in for two years. So Rosemary raised the subject once more with her brother.

"I've been talking to someone about fostering, Clayton. I know you're not sold on it, but there is a girl who needs a home. I know we're not a traditional family, and we don't know anything about kids these days, and it would be a big change for both of us. But maybe that would be a good thing. Am I being ridiculous?"

"No, not at all. Sounds like you're trying to convince yourself more than selling me on the idea. How about we just take that girl because we can?" Clayton replied. "Maybe we can help her. God knows we could have used someone helping us when we lost our parents at such a young age."

Rosemary hadn't expected that. Clayton rarely spoke of their loss. No one did, really. That seemed to be the way it was back then. An aunt they didn't even know simply

stepped up and gave them a place to live, plus three meals a day. When they were old enough, they came back to the empty family home and got on with things.

Rosemary pulled a loaf of brown bread from the bread maker. Being approved as foster parents had been a lengthy and challenging process once they made their decision. The waiting had only cemented her and Clayton's resolve to welcome the thirteen-year-old girl named Anne, who had spent her last five years in and out of several foster homes.

Rosemary walked to the bottom of the stairs and called up to Anne. "Lunch is almost ready. Come down and set the table, please."

Anne came into the kitchen and silently went about placing the cutlery, butter, and salt and pepper on the table. "The bread smells good," she said.

"We'll need bowls for the chili and small plates for our bread. When you're done, you can go out and tell Clayton lunch is ready." Rosemary looked up from slicing the bread and smiled as she watched Anne skip across the yard. Not for the first time, Rosemary realized how grateful she was to have a brother like Clayton. He had taken the whole fostering process in his stride and had a way of calming her whenever she became overwhelmed.

Out in the barn, Clayton stroked the calf as she rose to her wobbly feet. "She's pretty cute, ain't she?"

"Can I name her?" Anne knelt next to him.

"Of course you can."

"I'm going to call her Diana."

"Well, ain't that a fine name, now."

"You know lots about farming, don't you?" Anne settled into a cross-legged seat on the barn floor.

"Well, I guess I do. Don't know much else though."

"That's not true. You know a lot of the answers when we watch *Jeopardy!* You can tell the weather in your bones, and…you always know how to make me laugh." Anne reached out to pet the little calf, avoiding Clayton's thoughtful eyes. He cleared his throat and then chuckled.

"Not everyone gets my lame jokes, so I'm glad you like them. I don't usually have much of an audience, and Rosemary's heard them all over and over." Clayton began to place fresh bedding in the calf's stall as Anne remembered her reason for coming to the barn.

"Oh! I was supposed to tell you lunch was ready." She got to her feet and brushed loose hay off her clothes.

"I guess we'd better go in, then, shouldn't we? Maybe after lunch, you can give Diana her dose of medicine. She seems pretty calm around you."

"I like it here, you know. I know sometimes it seems like I don't, but I do. I'm glad I came here."

"The pleasure's all ours, Anne-girl."

Trudy Allan did indeed come by a few days later, as promised. She was enjoying one of Rosemary's molasses cookies when the school bus pulled up outside the house.

"Bus time already," Rosemary said as she poured more tea in Trudy's cup. "I'm never quite sure of the mood she'll be in when she walks through the door. Hope today's been a good day."

But Anne came stomping in the door, seemingly oblivious to the social worker sitting at the kitchen table.

"I am not going back to that school until Mr. Phillips apologizes. I had every right to break my slate over that horrid boy's head. Gilbert pulled my hair and called me Carrots. And I will not soon forget the humiliation of standing at that blackboard all afternoon. I will not be darkening the doors of that school until I have been justly exonerated!"

With that, Anne turned and left the kitchen, leaving both women speechless for a few seconds.

"Her teacher is a woman," Rosemary said weakly. "And I am quite sure they don't use slates these days. Even in my day, they were a thing of the past."

"She's got herself in a state, that's for sure," Trudy Allan said. "Maybe it's best I don't go after her just yet. We'll let her calm down. Has there been anything else about Anne's behaviour that's concerned you lately?"

Rosemary thought back to the strange conversation that had taken place at breakfast time that morning. Anne had asked some strange questions about her arrival and the circumstances around her placement, but until now, Rosemary hadn't thought it important enough to tell the social worker.

"She did ask some strange questions at breakfast time this morning," Rosemary said. "Anne asked me if she was carrying a tapestry bag when Matthew picked her up at the train station. And then she immediately switched to something else when I asked her who Matthew was."

"That is strange," Trudy said, "because Anne did not come here on a train."

"There's more. Then she said that she hadn't been very nice to Rachel the first time she met her." Rosemary continued her account of the strange conversation as Trudy sipped her tea and simply listened.

"I said, 'Do you mean Violet? You were quiet, as I recall.' Anne didn't answer but went on to say that Rachel said some horrid things to her and then got quite upset and said she couldn't help it if she was skinny and homely, had freckles, and had hair as red as carrots." Rosemary paused and looked over at Trudy.

"After Anne left for school, I asked Clayton his memory of that meeting in case I'd forgotten it somehow. He said he didn't remember her even talking to Violet that day."

Rosemary poured more tea into Trudy's cup and sighed.

"It's not just this morning's questions—it's some of the other things Anne says. Sometimes, I haven't got the vaguest idea of what she's on about. Yesterday, she said something about the day she dyed her hair green by accident. Clayton says I'm overreacting and that Anne just has an overactive imagination. But now, I'm not so sure. I'm not convinced that any of what she just told us actually happened at school today. If she's made it all up, that seems like a problem to me." Rosemary looked worried.

"Well, let's not jump to conclusions," Trudy said.

"Children have a way of exaggerating and over dramatizing things. Let's see what I can get out of her. We can always call the teacher later for her account. Thanks so much for the tea and the delicious cookies."

After Trudy left the room, Rosemary picked up the teacups and placed them in the dishpan. Maybe after Clayton heard about Anne's outburst, he'd take Rosemary's concerns seriously.

Trudy Allan walked quietly up the stairs. Standing in the upstairs hallway, she glanced over at the faded book sitting on the table. She knocked gently on Anne's bedroom door and opened the door a crack. Anne was lying face down on the bed.

"May I come in?" Trudy asked.

"Yes," Anne replied, turning over slightly. "I suppose I'm in trouble again."

"You aren't in trouble, Anne, but I'd like to talk to you. Seems you had an upsetting day at school today." Trudy perched on the edge of the bed.

"Nobody will believe me. They'll say I'm making it up." Anne punched a pillow and sat up.

"Making what up, Anne? Can you tell me what happened?" Trudy asked calmly.

"It doesn't matter. No one ever believes me when I tell them stuff. The last home I got kicked out of, no one believed that I thought I was serving Emily raspberry cordial." Anne sniffed.

"Anne, you and Emily drank a whole bottle of red wine. And you know that's not the only reason the

Wilsons asked to have you placed somewhere else." Trudy now spoke in a slightly firmer tone, which prompted Anne to sit up straighter.

"Are you placing me somewhere else again?" Anne looked directly at Trudy, who paused a moment before speaking again.

"No, I'm not. Rosemary and Clayton tell me you have been no problem. This school thing is the first trouble you've had, and I'm sure we can figure that out." Trudy stood up and smoothed creases out of the bed quilt.

"Well, I'm not going back there." Anne kicked the quilt.

"Raspberry cordial, Gilbert, and carrots. Is all this an *Anne of Green Gables* thing? I loved that book when I was your age." Trudy paused, but Anne only flopped back down on the bed and covered her head with the pillow.

After she returned downstairs, Trudy Allan sat down at the kitchen table across from Rosemary.

"I didn't get much out of her. She's pretty upset right now. I'm going to let her settle before I dig any further. Can you tell me about the book on the table at the top of the stairs? Has she read it, do you think?" Trudy wanted to know.

"I don't think so. I've never seen it move from the table. Anne noticed it right away the first day she arrived. I asked her if she liked to read, and I told her she was welcome to read it if she wanted. She seemed really upset by the book." Rosemary frowned, wondering if she and Clayton had made a terrible mistake in opening their

home to an obviously troubled teenager.

"I can't quite figure it out, but some of this seems all mixed up with that story. Are you familiar with it?" Trudy was now even more curious to get to the bottom of all the coincidences that she saw between the book and Anne.

Rosemary stood up and walked across the room. "Not really. It was my mother's favourite, and she always tried to get me to read it. I didn't want to, especially after she was gone. I keep the book on the table, though. A shrine, my brother calls it." Rosemary ran hot water into the dishpan and concentrated on the teacups.

"How old were you when your parents died, Rosemary?" Trudy asked thoughtfully.

Silence hung in the room, and it was several minutes before Rosemary sat back down and answered Trudy's question.

"I was ten, and Clayton was twelve."

"That must have been terrible for you both. Anne was eight when her parents were killed in a car accident. She was in the accident with them but was uninjured. Poor girl had no family, and this placement is the longest she's been anywhere." Trudy shared the sad story of Anne's past.

"We had a family—an aunt—and, believe me, we often wished we didn't. But at least we had each other." Rosemary picked up a dish towel from the rack and began drying the teacups.

"At least you had each other," Trudy repeated, watching Rosemary work. Then Trudy looked at her watch and reached for her jacket. "I really should be going. I'll check

with Anne's last social worker and see what she can tell me. I don't want to overreact, but it seems something more is going on with Anne. I certainly don't want to remove her from your home, as it seems this is the most settled she's been. Call me if anything else happens or any other behaviour concerns you."

Rosemary didn't have to wait long for the next strange episode with Anne.

"Do you have an amethyst brooch?" Anne wondered as she brought her lunch dishes to the sink for Rosemary to rinse, then plunked down at the kitchen table with an armload of homework.

"Pardon me?" Rosemary looked over at Anne.

"Amethyst. A purple stone. I Googled it. If you had one, I'm sure it would be pretty. I'd probably try it on and lose it, and then maybe you would think I stole it." Anne buried her math homework under her geography textbook.

"I don't know what you're going on about now." Rosemary threw the dish towel over her shoulder and sat down across from Anne.

"But I know you've got three pages of math to finish. I told your teacher I'd bring your homework to her later today. Clayton disagrees with me, but I think this staying home business is stupid. You just have to admit you made up the whole hair-pulling and name-calling incident and get yourself back to school where you belong."

"My punishment for taking the brooch was to apologize if I wanted to go to the Sunday School picnic."Anne

continued, unfazed.

"It's December, for heaven's sake," Rosemary said, raising her voice a bit. "Who has picnics in December? Besides, you don't even go to Sunday School."

"Maybe I should. I could pick flowers on my way there and cover my plain hat with buttercups and wild roses."

"Stop this ridiculous chatter, Anne, and get to work. You can dry the dishes when you finish your math. I'm going out to the barn."

Out in the barn, Clayton forked hay into the feeding troughs and listened to Rosemary's worried rant. "I don't know what is wrong with that girl. It's as if she's living in some fantasy world. She keeps asking me ridiculous questions and talking nonsense. Yesterday, she was all upset, saying she'd put anodyne liniment in her cake instead of vanilla. She hadn't even made a cake. What in the world is going on with that girl? I thought Mrs. Allan would have gotten back to us by now. Hopefully, she can find out something that explains Anne's strange behaviour."

Clayton hung up the hay fork and leaned against the barn wall. "I just think the girl's got a good imagination. She writes stories, you know. She told me yesterday she plans on starting a story club with her friends."

"What friends? She doesn't have any friends, and now that she isn't even going to school, the chances of her making any are slim. I am hoping Mrs. Allan can get her in to see a therapist again."

"Rosemary, don't you remember how much we hated

being dragged to head doctors? Anne just needs what we needed—time and a bit of understanding."

"I'm not sure if that's enough, Clayton. She's living in some other reality."

Three weeks later, Trudy Allan returned with a file folder, thick with papers. Rosemary opened the door, glad that Clayton had taken Anne with him for his weekly trip to the feed store in town. She put the kettle on and sat down to listen to whatever Trudy had to say.

"She's had a lot of intervention over the last five years, Rosemary. Five different social workers, four foster homes—not including yours—and she's seen three different therapists. Each one agrees that the trauma of seeing her parents die has affected Anne deeply, but that is as far as they go. One suggested medication, one group sports, and the other acupuncture, for heaven's sake. One foster home was overly strict, one was a zoo, the next was run like a sweatshop, and the last one tried but Anne's behaviour was out of control." Trudy flipped through page after page as she spoke.

"I sometimes wish Anne would act out," Rosemary said. "More and more, she's retreating into some made-up world. It breaks my heart how unhappy she seems and how hard she tries to convince us of the opposite."

"Has she said anything more about going back to school?"

"No, she is still sticking to her version of things and refuses to even talk about going back. Clayton is going right along with her. He says we just need to be patient

and give her time and understanding."

Later that day, Anne pulled up an overturned bucket and sat down near where Clayton was milking their one Jersey cow. The overhead light bulb cast a shadow in the dim light of dusk.

"I love the plinking sound the first few streams of milk make when they hit the empty metal pail," Clayton said. "Then I love the plop and spray as the pail fills up. Nothing quite like milking a cow to relax a person, I tell you. Seems old-fashioned the way I do it, I suppose, but it suits me."

Clayton kept milking, the silence between them broken only by the sound of the milk hitting the pail and the steady breathing of the contented cow. It was several minutes before Anne spoke.

"I don't feel like I'm in the right time," Anne said. "I feel like I'm Anne but a different one and living a long time ago before there was even electricity, motorcars, the internet, or television.

"Oh, way back. Even further back than when this old guy was your age. We had electric lights, and my dad had an old Chevy half-ton. No internet though and only two channels on a black-and-white TV," Clayton replied.

Silence settled again and a few minutes passed, the pail getting fuller.

"Want to try this, Anne?" Clayton asked as he stood and motioned for Anne to sit on the milking stool.

Anne sat down, waiting for instructions and courage.

"Pull from the top, gently squeezing your thumb and

first finger. It doesn't hurt her. Just get the feel of it."
Clayton demonstrated the technique. With his guidance,
Anne was able to extract some milk from each of the cow's
teats. It was much harder than it looked, and after a few
minutes, Clayton took over to finish.

"When I came to your house, it felt like I was coming
home. Does that sound weird?" Anne said, settling herself
on the floor, her back against the smooth worn boards of
the old barn.

"Not weird at all, Anne-girl," Clayton said. "I'm glad
you felt that way. It felt pretty good for Rosemary and me,
too. We didn't even know we needed a girl like you in our
lives until you showed up."

"I'm not too much trouble?" Anne's forehead creased as
she looked at Clayton.

"Too much trouble? Are you kidding?" Clayton moved
the milk pail out of the way and stood. He stroked the
cow as he unhooked the twine to release her tail.

"Why do you tie up the cow's tail?" Anne asked.

"It's the first thing I do before I sit to milk her. One
swish of that tail and you remember real quick and tie it
up. It doesn't hurt her to have a piece of baler twine
loosely fastened to her tail and hooked up to a nail on the
beam above her, but, believe me, it hurts if her tail hits
you sharply in the face."

Anne picked up the milking stool and returned it to its
place. Clayton picked up the milk pail, setting it out of
the way.

"We're almost done here, Anne. Let's just put the hay

out, and we can go in for supper."

Anne dragged a bale of hay across the floor, stopping in front of each animal's feed box, breaking off a flake for each.

Coming in for supper, Anne was bursting with excitement and could hardly get a bite in between sentences. "Clayton bought me some lined rubber boots that I can wear to do barn work. He got a new manure fork, too!"

"Well, isn't that great. Just the type of thing every teenage girl enjoys, I'm sure," Rosemary said sarcastically.

"I milked the cow, Rosemary! Clayton let me milk the cow. I didn't think I could do it. It felt so weird at first, pulling down on the teat. That's what Clayton called it—a *teat*. At first, I didn't even want to touch it. But he showed me how to squeeze down gently and get the milk to come from each teat. I caught on, and the milk really did come out into the pail. I even got so I could do two teats at a time. It's a lot of work and takes a lot of patience, just like Clayton said. But I did it!" Anne dug into her mashed potatoes, ravenous and bursting with pride

"I might lose my job," Clayton added. "She's a natural. Not everyone can get the knack of milking a cow."

"Well. Isn't that great? Milking cows and shovelling are things to add to your resumé for sure, once you get through school," Rosemary said. "Right now, you have a social studies project to finish. I let you take just the afternoon off to traipse around town with Clayton. You're not on holiday, you know."

Anne picked up her schoolbooks and headed upstairs.

"Sounds like you and Anne had a good afternoon,"

Rosemary said as she cleared the table. "Mine wasn't so good. Trudy Allan came by and gave me a heartbreaking account of Anne's last five years. Do you think we got more than we bargained for? Seems that girl needs a lot more than we can offer her."

"I don't believe that for one minute, Rosie. Anne simply needs what any of us need. Love for one and a place to belong. She told me today that our house felt like coming home, right from the start."

"It's not as easy as that, Clayton. She's got some serious problems. PTSD, Trudy calls it."

"PTSD. That's the buzzword these days, isn't it? But it's the same as it's always been. Terrible things happen, sad things that take the feet right out from under us. Bad stuff happens to folks, and they have to find a way to pick up the pieces. Seems to me our Anne-girl is doing her best to do just that. Just because social workers and shrinks don't understand her way of doing that, doesn't mean it's wrong." Clayton crossed his arms and leaned back in his chair defiantly, but Rosemary didn't back down.

"How exactly is she doing it, Mr. Knows-So-Much? Right now, Anne is hiding away in a house with two old people and, as far as I can see, is pretending to live a life that isn't hers."

"Time travel. I think she is pretending she's the girl in that book Mom loved." Clayton now pushed his chair back and got up from the table.

"That's ridiculous, Clayton. But what if she is? How is that a healthy thing, and what are we supposed to do with

that?" Rosemary stared at her brother and threw up her hands in exasperation.

"Maybe we need to read the book. Seems from what I remember from the TV show, Matthew and Marilla were able to take a sad and lonely girl and give her the life she deserved. That's the only fix, you know—having people who love you and accept you for exactly who you are." On that note, Clayton turned and left the kitchen.

The next day, Violet stopped by unexpectedly for an afternoon visit.

"I suppose you've heard that Anne isn't going to school these days. She's blown some imagined injustice right out of proportion, and Clayton doesn't think we should push the issue. Seems that Anne is getting her way, but even her social worker thinks we should let it play out." It didn't take long for Rosemary to bring up the matter most on her mind these days.

"I heard she hasn't been on the bus in a few days, but I didn't hear anything about an incident in school," was all Violet said in reply.

"Well, that's probably because there wasn't actually an incident. Anne made it all up." Rosemary took the teapot off the stove and walked toward the table.

"I think Anne's convinced herself she is Anne of Green Gables," Rosemary continued as she poured Violet a cup of tea.

"Kids do that kind of thing. My oldest granddaughter used to pretend she was Hermione after reading the entire Harry Potter series." Violet reached for the sugar.

"She stopped, though, right? And never really believed she was whoever that is." Rosemary pushed a plate of biscuits toward her friend.

"No, I suppose not. And yes, she's moved on to other books." Violet shrugged and reached for the plate.

"Clayton says we should read the book and just be patient with her. She's got to get back to school, though," Rosemary said.

"She'll get tired of staying home. Just let her enjoy being home on these days leading up to Christmas. It's probably a tough time of the year for her. You can push going back in January. I'm sure she'll be ready by then." Violet dipped a biscuit into her tea.

"I hope so. She came downstairs this morning with a huge story about nearly drowning when she was pushed out into Barry's Pond in a flat-bottomed dory." Rosemary shook her head and sighed.

"Just like what happened to Anne when she and her friends were imagining they were characters from Tennyson's poem," Violet said. "I've read *Anne of Green Gables* a few times myself. I can't believe you haven't."

"You're as bad as she is, for heaven's sake. I'll put her to work helping me to get ready for Christmas and see if it works. She might be glad to get back to school." With that, Rosemary concluded the discussion about Anne, and the two women compared notes about their Christmas shopping.

Rosemary was halfway through reading the copy of *Anne of Green Gables* Violet had lent her. Somehow it

didn't seem right to take the one off the table upstairs. Reading the book had been emotional all around, remembering her mother's love for the book and then realizing that so much of what Anne had been channelling since the day she'd arrived, came directly from the story.

"There's a chapter called 'Matthew Insists on Puffed Sleeves,'" Rosemary said, looking up from the book as Clayton came through the kitchen door. "The whole chapter is about Christmas, so I won't be surprised if Anne asks for a dress with puffed sleeves. I'm at a loss as to what to buy her, but I don't expect there'd be any such thing as a puffed sleeve dress in the stores these days.

"It is amazing just how accurate Anne is about things that happen in this book," Rosemary continued. "She must have read the book many times to remember all that she has."

"I think the human mind—the human imagination— is a pretty powerful thing, Rosie."

In the stillness of the quiet house several nights later, Clayton woke to a sound that at first didn't register. It took him seconds to realize what he was hearing, and in his sleepy state, he thought it was Rosie. Before shaking himself fully awake, he saw the kitchen as it looked fifty years ago and remembered the sound of his sister crying as he came in the door with an armload of wood. Dropping it in the woodbox that day, he'd known right away that Rosie's crying was because something bad had happened. Reverend Wilson and his wife never came by unless Mom was expecting them, and Mom and Dad had gone into

the city and weren't supposed to be back until dark.

Clayton stepped into the hall. The dropped flashlight made a long beam of light, but he saw Anne huddled in a dark corner. The quiet crying had intensified to a sob, and Anne did not look up as he approached but dropped the open book to the floor. Clayton silently sat himself down beside her and waited. Seconds later, Rosemary opened her bedroom door, and Clayton motioned for her to stay back. This type of crying was best left to peter out naturally, not stopped abruptly or managed in any way.

"I've been coming out here every night and reading this book," Anne said. "At first, it was because I was afraid I was forgetting parts, and if that happened, I couldn't keep pretending to be her. Then I realized that if I took some time every night to read it, I would feel like I was spending time with my mom and dad. But there were times in the last few days when I was so busy helping you in the barn, that I didn't even think about them. I stopped reading."

"Would it be so bad if you stopped pretending to be Anne of Green Gables?" Clayton asked gently.

"I had myself convinced that if I worked hard enough to pretend I was her, I could stop being me," Anne whispered. The crying started up again.

"Being you is okay, you know, Anne. We think you are a pretty special girl." Clayton moved to sit closer to her.

"I used to read parts of the book to my mom and dad whenever we went on long drives. They used to call me their little Anne of Green Gables." Anne wiped her eyes.

"You were reading to them that day, weren't you?" Clayton asked.

Anne's sobs started up again.

Clayton moved away slightly and took Anne's face in his hands. "The accident wasn't your fault, Anne."

Clayton reached for the flashlight and let the beam of light shine down on the discarded book. "I'm sure they loved you pretending to be Anne of Green Gables, but they loved the Anne who was their daughter so much more. It's time you started loving her, too. I know how much you miss them, but it's okay to be happy. They would want you to be happy."

"But I'll always miss them," Anne said, moving closer.

"Of course you will," Clayton said, touching Anne's hand.

"Even when I'm happy, I'm always still sad."

"I know." Clayton reached over and hugged Anne, and she lowered her head to his shoulder.

Rosemary walked quietly to the top of the stairs and switched on the downstairs hall light. "I'm going to put the kettle on," she said softly. "We'll have a late-night snack when you're ready."

Clayton's breath quickened as he caught sight of the store name in large letters above the doors. As he approached, he took in the colourful display in the store window and immediately felt overwhelmed. Adding to that anxiety were the several young teenagers who came

giggling out of the store and nearly ran him over. Clayton's panic intensified as he realized just from the window display that there were several styles and colours of jeans to choose from. He also really wasn't sure of Anne's size. What had made him think he could stroll into a women's clothing store and confidently purchase the right pair of blue jeans to give Anne for Christmas?

Instead, Clayton slipped into the nearby dollar store and quickly started filling his cart with miscellaneous items. No doubt Rosie could use a new wooden spoon, pot scrubbers, and some room deodorizers. He grabbed a few bags of candy and headed to the checkout. Even this store was causing him anxiety, so he knew avoiding the other one had been the right decision.

Clayton had driven halfway home before he was his own man again. Shopping had been a gruesome experience, but it served him right for thinking this was a task he could undertake. He needed a woman to handle this, and asking Rosemary was out of the question. She'd voiced her opinion many times on the ridiculous hole-riddled pants the kids were wearing these days. That left only Violet. Clayton put on the blinker and checked his blind spot before turning toward her house.

"Pick out blue jeans for you to give Anne? To be sure I will." Violet had been all too happy to help. "I'm going shopping tomorrow, and I'll attend to it. I could even buy them online, and they'd be delivered in lots of time. Do you have anything particular in mind? I know the styles vary. No? I'll go by my own judgment, then. Just leave it

with me."

"Thank you," was all Clayton said, eager to be gone. "Except…" He didn't know exactly what to say about the style he had seen on the girls coming out of the store.

"Don't you worry. I'll be sure they have rips all down the legs. I don't quite get it myself, buying brand-new jeans already peppered with holes, but I know that's what is fashionable these days. My own granddaughter has several holey pairs. I got after her at first, saying I could patch them for her, but that's the way they like them. I'll find a pair as holey as the best of them for our Anne."

The December night was bright, even with the light snow falling, as Clayton finished his barn chores. Anne had been out earlier but had hurried inside to help Rosemary finish wrapping some gifts and do some last-minute preparation for tomorrow's dinner. He was in no hurry to return to the house and get in the middle of any of Rosemary's Christmas frenzy.

He'd sit here awhile, instead, and let the soft breathing of the cows and the feel and smell of this old barn calm and steady him. Thinking back to the night he'd held Anne as she allowed the pain and anguish she'd carefully kept locked up for over five years to finally come out, he now let his own tears fall. He knew the pain of the impossible—the unimaginable—and he knew the sorrow that lingered. Even after fifty years, sorrow was a place he and Rosemary could so quickly return to and a place they honoured. He knew how important it was to remember the loss, but also knew the importance of allowing your-

self to heal and keep on living.

The barn door opened, startling Clayton, and he turned to see Anne approaching.

"Are you all right, Clayton?" Anne asked.

"You scared the life out of me! Yes, I'm fine. Just enjoying the quiet in my happy place, but glad to have you join me." He motioned for her to join him.

"I was turning my light out when I noticed the barn light was still on. I'd been reading the chapter where Matthew dies, and for a second, I panicked." Anne pulled up a milking stool and sat down.

"Glad you're reading the book with the lights on, Anne-girl, and not sneaking out into the hall to read that creepy old one." Clayton chuckled.

"Violet gave me a brand-new copy. It's got illustrations, and guess what? Anne doesn't look anything like me." Anne laughed with him.

"And tonight, the old guy doesn't die, Anne," Clayton reassured her. "We just need to hang our stockings and get ourselves to bed so that we can be up bright and early to see what Santa brought us."

"Remember that I've stopped believing in storybook characters, Clayton. I just want to see what's in that box from you." Anne leaned over to give him a jab with her elbow and grinned. "I don't suppose it's a brown sateen dress with puffed sleeves, by any chance?"

Clayton ruffled her hair and grinned right back. "You'll just have to wait and see. So let's turn out the lights and let these animals settle."

"Love you, Clayton."
"Love you, too, Anne-girl."

New Brunswick writer **Susan White** lives on the Kingston Peninsula (just outside Saint John), where she and her husband, Burton, raised four children and ran a small farm. She earned her BA and BEd at St. Thomas University and taught elementary school for 29 years. Susan retired in 2009 to write full time, and has published thirteen books. Her latest novel, *The Way I Feel,* was just released, and her first book, *The Year Mrs. Montague Cried,* won the Ann Connor Brimer Excellence in Children's Literature Award in 2012.

Find her online at: www.susanwhite.xyz

JUDITH GRAVES

Anne

She's off the rails.

To my kindred spirits, you know who you are.

The train clattered along the track, its shrill bursts of steam and grinding gears matching the snaps and misfires of Anne's internal wiring. Though they'd done their best to assess and repair the damage, the asylum simply wasn't equipped to deal with the intricate mechanisms of an *e* unit like her.

Especially one with battlefield experience. Anne fussed with the leather clasps on her handbag, grateful for its weight on her lap as it fixed her in place. In this world, she was nearly lost in memory.

If she had been capable of speech when she arrived at the asylum's imposing double doors, Anne would have saved them the trouble. A bit of time and her programming would mend what human hands could not. Once her restoration program was complete, she'd be all that she was, and then some.

Instead of a rush of relief, the thought stabbed her with fear. Anne placed a hand over her heart and stared out at the dust and decay slipping by the passenger car windows. The view sparked a sense of grief. So much had been lost. How did the pure humans do it? Go on every day at the mercy of emotions? She'd forgotten their raw strength.

Little wonder *e* units came with a detachment option.

How else could a human–AI hybrid with cybernetic physical enhancements complete duties and stay sane?

It appeared Anne would be the one to find out. Either she'd find a way to manage her newfound state, or she'd go mad and compromise her efforts to seek refuge in the neutral zone.

"You mustn't tell anyone what you are, not a single soul," the asylum matron had warned. Her body was lean and stooped with age, but her eyes were soft. She'd been kind from the first moment Anne had some level of awareness. And with that, so many questions.

"But what am I?" she'd asked, memories a whirling fog of anguish, bloodshed, and the shrill cries of the dying.

"A weapon. A secret." The matron's lips tightened for a moment, then relaxed into a wide smile. "And a spirited young thing who deserves a second chance." She spun Anne to face the long mirror embedded in the wardrobe door. "This red hair of yours will draw enough unwanted attention, best to keep it restrained." Parting Anne's thick locks down the middle, the matron set to work creating two simple plaits. When she finished, she eyed Anne's reflection. "You'll pass for twelve. Eleven if you're lucky. Never set that hair free, my dear, or the jig's up." She loosened the braids at the nape of Anne's neck. "Be sure to always hide the mark."

Anne gently traced the brand at the base of her hairline. A lowercase, italic *e* made of an intricate crosshatching of black lines: her model and serial number. The pattern unique to Anne, each *e* unit could be tracked and located with a single scan by one of the Magistrate's enforcers.

Once she was safe in Avonlea, an insignificant farming town deep in Providence's neutral zone, Anne just might be able to build a new life.

One without blood on her hands.

"Providence has its share of extremists too, mark my words." The matron brought reality back with the subtlety of a parasol spike to the temple. "The island may not be a target. Not yet, but how do you think it's gone unscathed this long? Those potato fields have many eyes, child. Best remember that as well. If even one of those hoe-wielding farmers discovers the truth, they'll turn on you like feral dogs."

Thus far, Anne had been able to keep up the pretense. Even earning the protection of the Providence Island Line train's elderly porter, a rotund man with a curling grey mustache and chronic worry buried in the frown lines that etched his face.

"I see you've spotted them," he said now, leaning over the back of her seat to peer out the window. Lost in her thoughts, Anne had indeed been observing the approaching riders but only now realized their context. Six men, their faces hidden under faded bandanas, raced on horseback alongside the locomotive.

Highwaymen.

Outlaws. Rebels against the Magistrate and all he stood for. They funded their cause by holding up trains, neutral

274

zone or not. Statistics and probability outcomes flooded Anne's network as suppressed military protocols surged and failed. Sharp stabs of fire lit through her mind. She clamped a hand over her mouth, holding back a wave of nausea.

"Not to worry," the porter said, misinterpreting her actions, likely guessing she was simply afraid.

And she was. But not of the would-be robbers. If her programming triggered, this journey would be well and truly over—for everyone onboard.

"Once we hit the double tracks, the conductor will initiate an Express order." The porter withdrew a small gold watch from his waistcoat pocket. "Any minute now…" The thunder of hooves drowned out the hiss of the train's steam engine, and the other travellers perked up and pressed their noses against the glass windows.

"They'll steal my new bear," a child's voice from a few rows ahead.

"Nonsense, son," his father said. "They're after the mail car or the treasury. Teddy's just fine."

But the muffled thuds of warning shots fired into the sky over the train had the passengers gasping in alarm. Their panic fuelled a surge of adrenaline in her blood, and, swift as a stallion's hoof to the face, Anne's vision expanded.

She scanned the landscape, ignoring the flood of geographic and exterior temperature data now in her peripheral, and focused on the immediate threat. Passengers nervously tracked three riders advancing to the mail car while Anne was keenly aware of the remaining high-wayman. Her thermal sensors revealed that he had slowed his horse to match the train's speed, dropped the reins, and leapt from the saddle.

He was climbing aboard.

Threat detected. Engage.

Anne stood and set her handbag on the embroidered cushion. "Excuse me," she mumbled, sliding from her seat, "I require the lavatory."

"You really shouldn't go now, miss." The porter glanced up from his watch, his brows furrowed. "Things get bumpy when we switch modes."

"That's what I'm afraid of." With one hand on her stomach and the other covering her mouth, Anne faked a dry heave. Then another.

"Oh dear." His eyes widened. "I don't want vomit in my car. The stench would be unbearable for patrons. Let her through," he announced, waving her into the crowded aisle. "Sick one coming through."

After that, no one blocked her escape to the back of the car and through to the vestibule connecting it to the next. When the doors closed behind her, Anne straightened from her stoop and smoothed her skirts.

Passengers paid her no mind, their bodies and faces pressed to the glass windows, tittering over the highway-men's progress. Taking advantage of their distraction, Anne collected a few objects as she glided through the next compartment.

A metal-tipped parasol.

A vial of smelling salts.

A tattered copy of last week's edition of *The Chronicle*. She did love to keep informed of the Magistrate's latest propaganda.

Sliding doors whooshed open to the next compartment just as her target dropped from a smoking hole in the roof. He rocked on his heels, off-balance by the blowtorch he held in one hand.

He staggered and tamped down the flame, unaware of the girl watching his every move.

Anne slipped the newspaper behind her and tucked it into the waistband of her skirt.

With a quick glance around, Anne assessed there were no passengers in the narrow corridor, waiting their turn to use the facilities.

Fortuitous.

She cleared her throat.

The highwayman's head snapped up. She admitted he made an intimidating sight. Stocky, broad-shouldered, and his features covered by a partial respirator. It was meant to filter the air and protect the wearer from the many airborne viruses contained in unfiltered oxygen.

Such a shame he hadn't invested in the more costly full-face version.

She struck fast, tossing the smelling salts directly into his exposed eyes. Stunned, he stumbled backward, dropping the torch at his feet. Anne calmly kicked it out of reach. It was so easy to be wicked when she wasn't bothered by pesky human emotion.

"It burns, it burns." The man frantically swiped his eyes, growling in agony as his efforts only spread the ammonia faster.

"I can fix that." In a blur of movement, Anne slapped his hands from his eyes and stabbed the parasol's metal tip into one socket, then the other.

Brutal. Yet efficient. An *e*-unit's calling card.

The highwayman dropped backward with the force of her thrusts. His head struck the wood floor with a sickening thwack, the parasol still embedded in his skull.

The entire incident took less than a minute. It took three more to shove the body back through the hole in the roof, the parasol coming in handy there as well. A good weapon serves more than one function.

Threat neutralized. Resume.

The world spun around her. A dull throb began at the base of Anne's skull.

Wait, what was she doing here, frozen in place and staring at the freshly mopped wood floor?

Anne sucked in a breath. Of course, she'd been feeling poorly, how silly to forget. Well, her guts were still as stone now. She shook off her confusion and exited the boxcar just as a rumbling built underfoot and the train swayed.

Clutching her handbag, Anne found her seat with the least fuss possible.

"Feeling better, miss?" A kindly woman asked from across the aisle.

"Much." Anne ignored the pain that had shifted to her

278

temples and forced a smile. "Would you like some reading for the journey?" She offered up the newspaper. Only a keen eye would detect the slight tremor in her fingers.

"Why, thank you, dear," the woman said. "I could use the distraction. So much trouble on trains these days. What is the world coming to?" She held the paper aloft and flipped through the pages.

What indeed?

A headline caught Anne's attention before slipping out of view. "Orphan asylum burns to dust in Halifax fire." For a moment, the stench of fire and burning flesh overwhelmed her. Oh no. The asylum. Burned to the ground. Had the matron survived? Had it been targeted deliberately?

One thing was certain, there was no turning back now. Her only place of refuge had been destroyed.

"Hold on," the porter called out, and Anne pressed the handbag tight to her chest—it was all she had left.

The entire car jolted and surged forward as the train launched into Express. Passengers who'd been foolish enough to stand and gape at the highwaymen were blasted back into their seats. In seconds, the riders were nothing more than black specks in the distance.

A rhythmic shimmy settled over the locomotive, and the sudden force eased.

"Three cheers for the conductor!" a man bellowed. Relieved laughter, along with a few appreciative rounds of applause, rang out from the passengers.

The porter gave Anne one last smile, then continued

along the aisle to check on the well-being of the other travellers.

It took much concentration to relax her grip on the handbag. Her knuckles had locked onto the fabric as if clenched around a weapon. Strange. That feeling was so familiar. As if she'd been in a battle recently, instead of many months ago.

If it ever became fully functional, her programming would dictate she return to the front lines. Precisely the reason Mrs. Spencer, head matron of the asylum, had hacked her system and deleted specific protocols. The attempt alone should have resulted in a full shutdown, but thanks to the bullet still lodged in the human portion of her brain—effectively scrambling key coding—the hack had been successful.

But at what cost?

Now that she could feel again and was bombarded with emotions at every turn, she wanted no more blood on her flesh-covered mechanical hands. Never again would she fight battles so long ago waged that no one remembered what they were fighting for. She was the first *e* to have free will with impunity.

Well, the first to her knowledge. Such infractions would hardly make front-page news. Not that the papers reported anything other than what the Magistrate wanted survivors to know.

"Avonlea Station, Avonlea," the porter called. The train chugged and huffed to a stop. Passengers chatted amiably as they gathered their personal belongings and exited from

the train car.

Dread clawed up Anne's spine as she made her way to the door. All she had to do was step down onto the platform and into a new life.

"Can I help you with that, miss?" A smiling gentleman in Providence uniform asked, holding out his hand for her carpetbag.

"No, thank you, sir," Anne said, twisting out of his reach and hopping from the train. "There's a knack to holding it, if you don't mind." She glanced over the near-empty platform. "It appears I'm to wait for my ride." The thought wasn't oppressive. Avonlea was a variable paradise. Gone were the wastelands of the outer provinces, replaced by lush grasses, strong and tall green trees, and a bright-blue sky as far as the eye could see. Bees hummed and birds chirped amongst the treetops. Instead of recycled oxygen, here the air smelled of sunshine and warm apple pie.

"Train's early," the stationmaster said. "Do you wish to go inside to the ladies' waiting room?"

Hope lodged firmly in Anne's heart. "I do believe I'll wait outside. Right there on that bench." She grinned. "So much more scope for the imagination, don't you agree?"

"I suppose…" the man muttered, but his doubt was lost on Anne, who'd already plunked down on the bench and was staring up into the heavens with unrestrained joy.

She had done it. She'd left pain and terror behind and stepped into the light. Nothing would take this new world from her. No thing. And no one. A tremulous smile

pulled at the corners of her mouth.

Avonlea had a new protector.

Lord save them all.

Judith Graves is an award-winning young adult fiction writer (*Exposed* and *Infiltrate:* Retribution Series with Orca Book Publishers), as well as a screenwriter and illustrator. *A Tale of Two Kitties*, her debut picture book, was published by Acorn Press. A firm believer that fiction can be action-packed, sassy, and yet hit the right emotional notes, Judith writes stories with attitude. As a child, Judith lived in Summerside when her father was in the Forces. It was a sad day when he was posted and the family moved to Alberta. She may have convinced her husband to have an *Anne of Green Gables*–themed wedding. The Island kept calling to Judith, and now, many years later, she's back and thrilled to be living in Summerside with her husband and sassy fur babies.

The ANNEthology Compiling Editor: **Judith Graves** entered her *ANNe* in a short story contest in 2013, run by the Surrey International Writers' Conference, and won in the Writing for Young People category. Having spent her early childhood living in Summerside, PEI, and growing up with *Anne of Green Gables*, Judith set a goal for herself to write something about Anne one day. A short piece of fiction seemed like a super way to dive into the Green Gables world, especially if she added a twist. Where would other authors take Anne? she wondered. Fast-forward to today, and her dream of asking other talented authors from all over the country to take Anne for a spin has finally come true. *The ANNEthology* is a fantastic collection of stories that showcases the depth and beauty of Anne's character—in a multitude of incarnations, written by talented authors. None of this would have happened without Natasha Deen's brilliant networking channels, Robin Sutherland's story editing insights, Hope Dalvay's copyediting polish, and, of course, Terrilee Bulger's support in producing *The ANNEthology* through Acorn Press, PEI's amazing publishing house. As Anne once said, "All things great are wound up with all things little." So true, Anne, so very true.

The ANNEthology General Editor: **Robin Sutherland** can't remember a time when she wasn't working with words: reading them, studying them, and teaching others how to use them. She holds a PhD in literature and a certificate in Technical Writing, and has worked variously as a university instructor, a writing centre coordinator, and a freelance writer and editor. Also a creative writer, she has recently completed a collection of stories based on her years as a lifeguard in the Toronto suburbs.

The original *Anne of Green Gables* has always been one of Robin's favourite books, so she was easily persuaded to serve as *The ANNEthology*'s story editor. What sorts of alternative Annes were out there? She definitely wanted to find out, and loved working with our ten writers as they mined familiar territory and tested (and often twisted) boundaries to accommodate the needs and voices of their new characters and plotlines. What a great way to pay homage to the timeless themes of friendship, family, home, creativity, and resilience that Lucy Maud Montgomery first introduced to us through Anne Shirley and the world of Green Gables.

Thanks for reading!

If you've enjoyed this book,
please visit our website for other reads.

www.acornpresscanada.com